BELLY FLOP

Born in the UK, Morris Gleitzman moved to Australia with his family at the age of sixteen. His career took off as a screenwriter and a newspaper columnist, before he became a successful author. He has written a number of children's books, including *Two Weeks with the Queen*, *Water Wings*, *Blabber Mouth* and *Sticky Beak*. He lives in Melbourne and has two children.

Visit Morris Gleitzman's website
at www.morrisgleitzman.com

Praise for *Belly Flop*:

'Morris Gleitzman is a very funny writer, and *Belly Flop* is moving as well as funny. Just when the reader thinks the jokey, bravado atmosphere is coasting along, it shifts gear and heads for a cataclysmic denouement.'
TES

'A gripping, amusing and rather moving story.'
Mail on Sunday

'A hard-hitting, often nail-biting story.'
Independent on Sunday

'*Belly Flop* combines insight with snappy humour and an eye for what makes people tick . . . a shrewd novelist, wise to the psychology of young minds.'
Scotland on Sunday

Morris Gleitzman

Belly Flop

MACMILLAN
CHILDREN'S BOOKS

First published 1996 by Pan Macmillan Publishers Australia
First published in the UK 1996 by Pan Macmillan Children's Books

This edition published 2001 by Macmillan Children's Books
a division of Pan Macmillan Limited
20 New Wharf Road, London N1 9RR
Basingstoke and Oxford
www.panmacmillan.com

Associated companies throughout the world

ISBN 0 330 39824 5

A CIP catalogue record for this book is available from
the British Library.

Printed and bound in Great Britain by Mackays of Chatham plc, Kent

For Mary-Anne

G'day Doug.

It's me, Mitch Webber.

Sorry to interrupt out of the blue like this, but I'm desperate.

Troy and Brent Malley are after me.

They're the toughest kids in town and I've never seen them so ropeable.

It's really Dad they're angry with, but they've decided to take it out on me.

If they catch me I'll be history.

They've got tractor starter handles.

Oh no, I'm getting a cramp in the leg from running.

Doug, I know it's been a long time, but you're the only angel I know.

Help.

My leg cramp's getting worse, Doug.

I can't run much further.

Sorry to pester you, but the Malleys are getting closer.

1

I know angels have got busy schedules.

I know you're probably in the middle of a dangerous flight or a complicated rescue or morning tea.

I know it must be a real pain having someone chucking their thoughts at you like this without an appointment.

Specially if you've just settled back on a cloud, taken the weight off your wings and slipped your boots off.

But it's really urgent, Doug, honest.

My lungs are nearly cactus.

The Malleys are so near I can hear the snot rattling in Brent's nose.

I need you.

Jeez, that was close.

When I slipped in that horse poo outside the newsagents, I thought I was Malley meat for sure.

Sometimes it's not so bad having small muscles.

If I had big ones like the Malleys, I'd never have been able to squeeze through that hole in the fence.

Troy and Brent are back there now, yelling.

They're arguing about whether to rip a bigger hole in the fence with their hands or climb over.

Once they decide, I'm dingo bait.

I need a hiding place, Doug.

That's the problem with living in a town with only seven shops, one pub, one bank, one service station and no thick forests.

There aren't many good places to hide.

The safe in the bank'd be good, but it's Sunday.

Even if it wasn't, Mum and Dad work there and I wouldn't want to aggravate Dad's stress rash.

It'll have to be the Memorial Park.

Hope my legs can make it.

This town's so remote, even if the Malleys only manage to inflict surface injuries I'll probably still cark it before the air ambulance arrives.

Now I'm up a tree and I can catch my breath, a thought's just hit me.

You probably don't even remember who I am, Doug.

You angels probably look after so many kids the details get fuzzy.

It's Mitch spelt M-I-T-C-H, Webber spelt W-E-B-B-E-R.

I'm the one who got my head stuck in the bars of that cattle truck.

At the Gas 'N' Gobble when I was little.

When I asked you for help you made the driver drop his ice-cream outside the Men's

3

so when he bent down to pick it up he saw my legs dangling under the truck and didn't jump into the cab and roar off and drag me halfway across Australia.

I think I was wearing a blue T-shirt.

It probably had burn marks on it from when I did that magic trick with the oven lighter and the fluff from under Gran's bed. The one where I asked you to put me out and you made Gavin Sims chuck his milkshake over me.

Do angels have secretaries? If you do, perhaps you could ask yours to jog your memory.

I've thought of trying to get in touch with you heaps of times lately, Doug, but each time I stopped myself on account of me probably being too old now and you probably being up to your neck in angel work.

I'm not stopping myself now, but, because I'm desperate.

You can probably tell that by how hard I'm thinking these thoughts.

And how hard I'm hoping you're receiving them, wherever you are.

Things are pretty crook here, Doug, and I can't manage on my own any more.

I need your help.

I understand if you can't fit me in immediately because you're busy rescuing a little kid from an iceberg or making a crocodile spit out a toddler.

But I'm hoping you're not, Doug.

Because Troy and Brent Malley are over there by the war memorial.

And they've spotted me.

I suppose a tree wasn't such a great hiding place when there are only three in the whole park.

I'm jumping.

I'm rolling in the dust.

I'm running.

Doug, protect me like you used to, please.

I thought I was a goner then.

If I'd taken another half a second getting across the main street that road train would have flattened me.

I'm not sure what'd be worse, being pounded by Troy and Brent Malley or being flattened by a ninety-tonne road train.

I was glad it came along, but.

The Malleys had to wait for it to pass, which gave me time to duck in here.

The dunnies at the Gas 'N' Gobble.

It's OK, Doug, it's not as obvious a hiding place as it sounds.

I'm a boy and I'm in the Ladies.

If anyone comes in I'll tell them I'm looking for the cigarette lighter Gran lost a couple of months ago.

Hang about, Doug.

Of course.

If you don't remember me, you must remember Gran.

She was the one who told me about you, when I was little.

She's tall and sort of wrinkled and she's got a bad . . .

Oh no.

The Malleys are next door in the Men's.

They've heard me panting for breath.

Here we go again.

I've never been that good at athletics, but I reckon if sprinting through a service station and jumping over petrol pump hoses was a school event, I'd be in with a chance.

Specially if I had very angry twins chasing me.

I thought Mr Kee the manager was gunna grab me, but he just stood there with his mouth open.

He didn't even say anything when Troy ran into a car door and dented it.

Or when Brent tripped over the air hose and landed in someone's shopping.

For a sec, when I glanced back, I thought that was you making all that happen, Doug.

Then I remembered what Gran used to tell me about you.

'He's not like one of those posh guardian

angels in the Bible,' she used to say. 'Doug's invisible, he doesn't do violence and he's very busy, so if you need him you've got to ask.'

I'm asking now, Doug.

The Malleys are getting close again.

I can hear them yelling round the corner.

I've just ducked down the side of Conkey's Store, but I doubt if that'll throw them for long.

You're probably wondering, Doug, why I'm not asking anyone around here for help.

Why I'm not running into houses and yelling 'neighbourhood watch' or something.

Things have changed since I last gave you a hoi, Doug.

Everyone in town hates me now.

They hate Dad and Mum and Gran too.

I'll explain why when I've finished climbing up into Mr Conkey's old storage shed.

Sorry that took a while, Doug.

It's really hard climbing wood when it's rotting.

I'm hoping the Malleys won't think of looking all the way up here in the rafters.

With a bit of luck.

Or rather with a bit of help from you, Doug.

Luck's something we haven't had much of around here lately.

Remember how last time you were round this way it hadn't rained for nearly four years? Well, we haven't had a sprinkle for eight years now, except for a few drops last January which everyone reckoned was from a leaky dunny on a Qantas jet.

It's a really crook drought, everyone says so.

Sheena Bullock's dog can unscrew after-shave bottles with its teeth, that's how crook a drought it is.

Everyone's suffering, but Dad's copping it the worst.

Remember how he used to be one of the most popular blokes in town, partly because of his sweet nature and partly because drought-struck farmers knew that if they came to see Dad he'd make sure the bank lent them some money to keep them going?

Well now everyone hates him.

Someone spat on him in the street yesterday. It was terrible. They'd been eating beetroot.

I've tried to explain to people that Dad's just doing his job.

That it's what a Bank Liaison Officer has to do, write reports on families who are going broke because the drought's killed their sheep and dried up their paddocks.

That's it's not his fault the bank gets twitchy when broke families can't pay back the money they've borrowed.

That it's not his fault the bank takes their farms instead.

I've told people a million times how much Dad hates writing those reports.

How he wishes he could be a swimming pool attendant like Grandad used to be.

How he'd give his right arm to . . .

Hang on, what's that noise?

~

For a sec I thought it was the Malleys climbing up to get me.

Relax, Doug, it was just the wooden beams expanding in the heat.

I'm lying stretched out on a rafter now so even if Troy and Brent do come into the shed they definitely won't be able to see me up here under the roof.

Where was I?

Oh, yes.

I'm always reminding people that Dad's the same kind bloke he was before the drought. Reminding them how he nursed the Bullocks' dog back to health after we found it in our backyard with bubbles coming out of its mouth.

But every time the bank chucks a family off their land, everyone blames Dad.

I tell them he's as upset about it as they are.

He is, he's got flaky skin on his upper thighs from the stress. (I don't tell them that.)

I tell them it's the bank bosses in the city that chuck people off their land, not Dad.

But they don't listen.

They just turn away and pretend I'm a bus stop.

Which is pretty hurtful, cause our town hasn't got any bus stops.

People are starting to hate Mum too, and all she does is work in the bank and cash drought–relief cheques and make cups of tea for people who are depressed and upset at the state of their sheep.

The bank offered to promote her to manager, but she said no cause she knew she'd cop it even worse.

Even Gran gets picked on when she goes shopping.

Well, she reckons she does.

She reckons someone muttered to her in Conkey's yesterday how they were going to slit her throat and reach in and pull her intestines out, but she was standing next to a noisy soft drink cabinet and her hearing's not the best.

Anyway, Gran's pretty tough.

It's Dad I'm most worried about, Doug.

If kids chuck my bag on the roof I can climb up and get it, but Dad can't if his clients do that to him. He's too overweight to be a good climber, plus he's meant to be resting his thighs.

The other kids do chuck my bag around a fair bit.

I reckon they hate me almost as much as their parents hate Dad.

I've tried not to think about it too much.

Until this arvo.

I nipped down to Conkey's for some corn chips.

11

Troy and Brent Malley were waiting for me.

When I saw the expressions on their faces and the tractor starter handles in their hands, I knew my worst nightmare had come true.

If only Dad had warned me the bank was gunna chuck the Malleys off their land.

I could have taken precautions.

Like staying indoors.

And I wouldn't have had to disturb you, Doug.

Sorry if I'm messing up your work schedule and causing you job-related stress, but I'm . . .

Listen.

It's that noise again.

That's not beams expanding, that's . . .

Oh, no.

Doug.

The Malleys are up here.

They must have climbed up the back of the shed.

They've just stepped out from behind an old crate and they're coming towards me along the rafter.

Grinning.

Their grins are even scarier than their scowls.

Doug, help, I'm on a thin strip of wood miles from the ground being stalked by killer twins.

12

There's only one thing I can do.

Jump onto the next rafter.

Doug, if you're there, could you give me a sign?

So I know you're looking after me and I won't fall and get mashed.

Just something small.

A thumbs up made of dust floating in the air.

A spider winking at me.

Anything.

Too late.

The Malleys are lunging at me.

I'm jumping.

I've made it.

I'm on the other rafter.

No I'm not.

The wood's splintering.

I'm falling.

Doug . . .

I'm not dead.

I can move both my arms.

And both my legs.

And most of my bottom.

Doug, you did it.

You broke my fall.

Jeez, I'd forgotten how good you are at this angel caper.

It must take years of training to make a

person who's falling that distance land exactly on a pile of empty cardboard boxes and not on the concrete floor or the rusty old sheep feed machine.

Thanks, Doug.

Troy and Brent can't believe it.

They're staring down with their jaws hanging loose.

Even from this far away I can see that their faces have gone pale and their legs are quivering.

They look like stunned sheep.

I'm shaking too.

On the inside as well.

My heart and liver and guts are quivering more than the stuff in the butcher's window when a cattle truck goes past.

Not because of the fall, Doug.

Because I'm so happy and excited.

You've come back.

It's amazing, Doug.

Now I'm a client of yours again, I feel totally different.

I can even run faster.

I've just made it home in a couple of ticks and the Malleys weren't even in sight.

Thanks, Doug.

Thank you.

Thank you.

Thank you.

This is the best birthday present I've ever had.

Did I mention today's my birthday?

That's why I'm catching my breath on the front verandah.

I don't want to burst into the house panting and looking like I've just been chased three times round town by a pair of psychopaths.

Mum and Dad have got enough stress as it is.

And they're about to have some more.

My birthday party starts in twenty minutes

and there's something about it I haven't told them yet.

Something very important.

I haven't been game to tell them in case they chucked a fit.

But now you're back, Doug, it'll be fine.

What I've got to tell them is that my birthday party's not just a birthday party.

It's the event that's gunna make everything in our lives OK again.

When I got inside, Gran was having a go at Dad as usual.

'Three more families heaved off their land by that bank of yours,' she was saying. 'Don't take it personally, but I reckon you're lower than the flap of skin on a sheep's rear end.'

Dad was ignoring her as usual and pretending to look for something in his briefcase.

'Mum,' said Mum wearily to Gran, 'do us all a favour and change the subject, eh?'

Gran got herself a beer.

Mum plonked a bowl of taco dip down with the other party food and then saw me.

'Mitch,' she said, 'we were wondering where you were. Did you get the extra corn chips?'

I tried desperately to think of an answer that wasn't a lie.

'Couldn't,' I said. 'Sorry.'

16

Mum ran a worried eye over the food table.

'Oh well,' she said, 'we should have enough.'

I took a deep breath.

I don't know if you were ever a kid, Doug, but if you were you'll know how hard it can be telling your parents stuff that might hinder their breathing.

'Mum,' I said, 'I've invited some extra kids to the party.'

Mum frowned.

'I thought we agreed,' she said. 'Five or six and no horses in the house.'

'Too many and it'll put a strain on the furniture,' said Dad, 'and the dunny.'

I took another deep breath.

'I've invited a few more than five or six,' I said.

'How many?' said Gran through a mouthful of peanuts.

'Seventy-three,' I said.

Mum dropped a plate of chocolate crackles.

Dad went so stressed he looked like a city person.

Gran had a coughing fit and sprayed peanuts across the room.

'I did it for all of us,' I said, banging Gran on the back. 'So we can show them our human side.'

Mum and Dad stared at me.

'That's why I asked you to rehearse your card tricks, Gran,' I went on, 'and you to learn some good jokes, Mum, and you to practise juggling ping-pong balls with your mouth, Dad. When all the kids see how much fun we are at parties, they'll tell their parents and everyone'll stop hating us so much.'

Dad jumped out of his chair so fast you'd never guess he's a bit overweight.

'Mitch,' he said, grabbing me and knocking the tomato sauce bottle over, 'stop that talk. The people in this town don't hate us. They just get crook with me because of my job. They certainly don't hate you. You're a good kid and it's just your bad luck to have me as a dad.'

I couldn't speak, partly because what he'd just said had made my throat go funny and partly because he was gripping my shoulders so hard.

If I hadn't already known him I'd have been amazed to discover he was a Bank Liaison Officer and not a professional arm wrestler.

There was another pause while Gran wiped tomato sauce off the jelly and Mum gave Dad a worried squeeze.

Then I told Dad he was wrong about the bad luck and that he was the only dad I'd ever want, even if we lived in a huge city where there were millions of other dads.

I put my arms round him as far as I could
and gave him a hug.

He is wrong, but.

Not just about me, about all of us.

We're the most hated family in the district.

Dad knows it.

That's why a tear ran down his face and
sploshed into Gran's beer.

And that's why I've invited every kid in
town to my party.

We're all sitting here watching the chocolate crackles melt and waiting for the kids to arrive.

They should be here any minute.

Mum and Dad have just had a private conversation in the kitchen and they don't seem so worried now about the extra kids.

When Mum and Dad came back in I had a thought.

'Let's drag my bed in,' I said, 'for the kids at the back to stand on so they can see the card tricks and the ping-pong balls.'

Mum and Dad looked at each other.

I think they could see the sense in it.

'And we'd better put some more mashed baked beans in the taco dip,' I said.

'Good idea,' said Mum. 'We'll do it after they get here.'

Dad nodded and spilled his tea.

I think we're all pretty excited.

Except Gran.

She seems to be frowning a lot, though that

could because her cigarette ash has dropped
down inside her bra.

They shouldn't be much longer now, Doug.
   You probably think I'm a bit mental, having
a party when everyone hates me.
   I'm not.
   I've thought about this for weeks and I
reckon it's a good plan.
   You work with kids, Doug, so be honest.
   What kid can resist a party?
   None in this town, it's a known fact.
   Plus I've made it really easy for them.
   I hand-delivered the invitations to their
school lockers so they wouldn't have to make
conversation with me.
   I chose three o'clock as the starting time so
they wouldn't have to gobble their lunch.
   And I made it fancy dress so they could
come in disguise if they were embarrassed to
be seen here.
   They'll arrive soon, you wait and see.
   Oops.
   Gran's choking on a Cheezel.
   I'd better go and bang her on the back.

Hope you don't mind me sending my
thoughts to you like this, Doug.
   It helps me keep my mind off the clock.
   If me yakking on like this is making it hard

for you to concentrate on saving any of the other kids on your roster, don't listen, OK?

It's twenty-seven past three.

Mum and Dad are looking a bit stressed.

Pity angels only do rescues.

We could do with something to break the tension and give us a laugh.

One of the balloons popping or Dad sitting on the pikelets or something.

Dad's been showing me the features of the calculator they gave me for my birthday.

'Look,' he said, 'it calculates loan repayments to six decimal places.'

Gran had a coughing fit.

I decided I'd better try and help everyone relax.

'Don't worry,' I said, 'the kids have probably been held up.'

'I doubt it,' said Gran, 'seeing as it only takes thirteen and a half minutes to walk from one end of town to the other, fourteen in a dust storm.'

Poor old Gran.

She gets a bit grumpy sometimes.

It's from being ancient.

I reckon she's remarkable for her age, but she does have one habit that gets her into a bit of strife.

Remember how she's always been a heavy smoker, Doug?

Well now she eats while she does it.

I don't blame her, but.

If I was in my twilight years I'd want to pack as much as I could into each moment too. I'd probably do something dopey like watch videos in the shower.

There goes Gran now, puffing away and choking on a chocolate crackle.

She's always choking on chocolate crackles.

It's her fault, she knows she should pour hot milk on them first. She knows they don't get soft enough when she dips them in her beer.

What makes it worse is she's pretty tall for an old person so she's got long pipes. That means when food gets stuck it's got a fair distance to travel and she needs a lot of thumps on the back.

It's OK but, she's pretty solid.

S'cuse me Doug.

It's nineteen minutes to four.

Mum and Dad are looking very stressed.

Dad's put his elbow in his beer three times.

A couple of secs ago a thought hit me.

Perhaps they're worried that when the kids arrive, they might all try to bash me up.

'It's OK,' I said, 'if things get out of hand I can give Doug a hoi.'

Mum and Dad looked at each other and pretended they hadn't heard.

'I probably won't have to,' I said, 'but he's around if I need him.'

Gran coughed a Cheezel across the room.

Mum and Dad looked at each other again and I could tell from their pained expressions they'd heard.

That's when I remembered.

Don't be offended Doug, but Mum and Dad don't believe in you.

It's one of their few real faults.

If they can't see a person, and offer them a cup of tea or something cold, they don't believe in them.

Try not to hold it against them, Doug.

It's seventeen minutes to four.

If a spaceship's landed in Memorial Park and everyone's down there, you'd let me know, eh Doug?

It's OK, Doug, I'm not crying.

My eyes are just a bit drippy, that's all.

Us humans get drippy eyes sometimes if we're tired or we've been watching too much telly or we get toothpaste in them.

Or we have a birthday party and nobody comes.

I still can't believe it.

I wasn't expecting every kid in town to trample the door down, but I thought some'd turn up even if it was just to see Gran cough bits of corn chip out of her nose.

Not a single one.

Not even Andy Howard, who'd normally walk naked through bull ants for a free feed.

Poor old Mum and Dad, it was good of them to try and cheer me up, even if they aren't very good at it.

Just now, when Mum said 'Never mind, love, they've probably got the wrong day', and Dad stared at the Cheezel on top of the TV and said 'They'll probably turn up next Sunday', I had to bite my tongue really hard.

I wanted to yell something really angry.

Something about how some parents' jobs make it really hard for a kid to have a birthday party.

I still do, but Gran's coughing and they probably won't hear me.

Anyway, it wouldn't be fair.

Dad can't help . . .

What was that?

Doug, quick.

The window just exploded.

There's glass everywhere.

What's happening?

Is someone shooting at us?

Are there farmers out there with guns?

Doug.

Help.

HELP.

25

It's OK Doug, it was just a brick.

Don't get me wrong.

That's bad enough.

We've never had a brick before and we're all shaking like a truckie's gut.

But at least it's not as bad as a bullet.

I just wish I'd seen it coming, then I could have got you to stop it.

But I didn't see it till it had smashed through the window.

The noise made us freeze and we just sat there like stunned fish fillets watching the brick land in the Cheezels and bits of glass bounce off the walls and tinkle across the floor.

Then everyone moved.

Mum dived protectively across Gran.

It was good of her, but a bit of a waste of time cause she's about half the size of Gran and her skin is still quite soft except for her elbows and Gran's is like leather-grain vinyl.

Still, you can't blame her for trying.

She's got diving in her blood from Grandad.

Poor old Dad hasn't.

When he tried to throw himself protectively on top of me he got the angle wrong and bounced off the rocker recliner and landed on the food table.

That's when I unfroze and yelled for you, Doug.

I know guardian angels are really only meant to protect kids, so it was good of you to make sure Dad's head missed the cutlery and landed on something soft.

All those swear words he came out with while we were getting the taco dip out of his eyes weren't about you, I promise.

They were about the person who chucked the brick.

We're out in the street now, but we can't see anyone.

Doesn't matter.

We know who did it, don't we Doug?

I've just told Mum and Dad about Troy and Brent Malley.

They were pretty shocked.

Mum gave me a hug.

Dad looked as though he was going to cry, though that might have been because of what he'd just seen.

27

My calculator.

Smashed to bits.

Dad reckons we mustn't jump to conclusions, but.

He could be right.

I've just noticed something scratched on the brick.

The word MONGREL.

I'm not sure if Troy and Brent Malley can spell that well.

Dad's on the phone now giving Sergeant Crean a list of the people he reckons would chuck a brick through our window. Dad hates dobbing, but he's had to mention most of the town.

I'm still shaking, Doug.

My guts feel like they've been through a sheep feed machine.

Mum's still shaking too. Even her shoulders are trembling, and I don't think it's because she's picking up broken glass. She's normally very relaxed handling sharp objects, that's why she's so good at darts.

Gran usually shakes a bit, but not as much as she is now.

She wouldn't admit it, but I think she's a bit scared. You can tell by the words she's yelling at Dad.

'Get a different job, Hopeless, before we're all killed,' for example.

Normally she's much ruder to him than that.

Mum and Dad have gone to give a statement about the brick to Sergeant Crean down at the bowls club.

Poor things.

It won't be easy for them, walking into that place with everyone throwing glances at them and muttering things.

I'm on my bed trying to fit my calculator back together.

It's not easy with my hands shaking so much.

Gran's just been in.

'Good on you for having a punt,' she said.

At first I thought she meant the calculator.

I'd just spent ten minutes trying to straighten a bent battery terminal and wondering if angels are any good at electrical repairs.

She didn't.

'That was a brave try, the party,' she said. 'You had a punt, that's the main thing.'

Gran reckons if a person won't have a punt, they might as well just lie down and let a cattle truck run over them.

'Thanks, Gran,' I said.

She went to her room for a rest.

Poor thing.

She's too old to be hated by an entire town.

Specially when her and Grandad used to be so popular.

Once Gran was president of the bowls club four years in a row.

And Grandad, before he died, was the most loved swimming pool attendant this town's ever had.

And the best diver.

It says so on his retirement medal.

The one Mum keeps in her bedside drawer for when she needs a cry.

I'm gunna stop wasting my time on this calculator, Doug.

I've got more important stuff to do.

Like come up with another plan to make everything in our lives OK again.

Last night wasn't a good night for coming up with plans.

My brain kept getting distracted by other stuff.

Worrying about school today, mostly.

Having to face all those kids.

Specially two of them in particular.

I'd have been awake all night if it hadn't been for you, Doug.

When I was little and Gran used to tell me about you, she always reckoned guardian angels were better than hot milk drinks for getting to sleep.

She was right.

Thanks, Doug.

I feel a bit better about the Malleys this morning.

I think it's because I dreamed about you, just like I used to.

Boy, I was glad to see you.

Well, not actually see you of course, but feel your breeze.

It was a top dream.

I was in the main street and I was pretty upset, partly cause Dad had just stuck his elbow in my ice-cream and partly cause the town was surrounded by hundreds of angry farmers with guns who wanted to kill us.

Me and Dad knew we were history.

Even if we ran as fast as we could, there was no way we'd make it to Conkey's, buy guns for ourselves, unwrap them and load them before the farmers started firing.

I wanted Dad to hold my hand tight, but he was busy wiping peach and mango ripple off his elbow.

Then the posters started flapping outside the newsagents and I knew it was you, Doug.

As usual you were amazing. In less than thirty seconds the farmers remembered some urgent fence repairs they had to do and went home in an orderly manner.

And I've woken up with a really good feeling.

That ripper peaceful feeling of knowing you're looking after me.

Emergency call to Doug.
Emergency call to Doug.
Dad's in a bad way.
I've never seen him so clumsy.
He usually has one accident on his way to

the car, maybe two, but I've never seen him have four.

Getting his keys tangled up in his hanky, dropping his briefcase, tripping over the garden hose and banging his knee on the carport all on the same morning'd be a record, I'd say.

I was at the mail box when he came a cropper over the hose, which he'd have to be pretty tense to do as it's been in the same spot untouched for eight years.

Then, when he was in the car, I understood.

Mum came out and before she got in the car herself she asked him if he needed some goanna oil for his knee.

'I'll be right,' he said. 'I'll just be doing desk work most of the day. I'm not due out at the Malleys with their eviction papers till three.'

My insides plummeted.

I went stiff with shock.

If there had been any birthday cards for me I'd probably have dropped them.

Mr and Mrs Malley are just as muscly as Troy and Brent, and taller, and they own about six guns each.

They shoot things for fun, not just sick sheep.

Doug, I know you're busy and I know guardian angels are really only meant to look after kids, but could you keep an eye on Dad this arvo?

33

He needs you, Doug.

Don't worry about me.

I'll have come up with a plan by then to win the hearts of everyone in town, including Troy and Brent Malley.

I know I will.

Thanks, Doug.

By the time I got to school I was so tense I couldn't think straight.

I couldn't stop imagining Dad's bullet-riddled body stuffed in the Malleys' sock drawer.

It took me a couple of minutes to notice Troy and Brent weren't around.

Even then I had the awful thought that perhaps they'd been kept at home to help load the guns so Mr and Mrs Malley won't have to stop to do it this arvo and lose concentration while they're shooting at Dad.

Then I realised it wasn't that, it was you, Doug.

You've made Troy and Brent late so I can get into class in one piece.

Simple and clever.

Which is also how I'd describe the idea I've just had, even though I say it myself.

It came to me while I was hanging up my bag.

I saw the permission form for the school excursion sticking out the top.

Have I told you about the school excursion?

A school way over on the coast has invited our school to go and take part in their swimming carnival on account of us being drought-struck. Someone must have told them about us not having any water in our town pool for the last eight years.

I was meant to get Mum or Dad to fill out the form over the weekend.

Poop, I thought when I saw it, and started filling it out myself.

Then the idea hit me.

The bus trip to the coast is gunna take about a million hours.

Kids get bored to death on buses.

So I'll have my party on the bus.

Pretty good, eh?

Most of the party food'll keep in the freezer till then and I can get Mum and Gran and Dad to teach me the jokes and card tricks and ping-pong ball juggling.

I'm on my way into class now.

I can't wait to tell everyone.

I reckon they'll be really grateful.

They'd have to really hate someone to knock back the chance of a long bus trip with no boredom and heaps of chocolate crackles and taco dip.

I don't reckon even they hate me that much.

~

They hate me that much.

I remembered they did the moment I walked into class and saw them all crowded round my desk.

And saw what was waiting for me.

A present, wrapped in shiny paper with a frilly bow.

And a card saying 'Happy Birthday Webface, hope you had a good party.'

I'd have ignored it if Mr Tristos hadn't walked in at that moment and seen it.

'Mitch,' he said, looking surprised, 'you're popular today.'

The kids started chanting 'Open it! Open it!'

I gave Mr Tristos a pleading look.

He doesn't usually let kids open presents in class and I was hoping desperately he'd stop me.

'Go on, Mitch,' he said, 'open it.'

Then I remembered that last year the bank chucked his wife's parents off their farm.

The kids cheered and Mr Tristos said he reckoned it was socks and the kids kacked themselves.

The smell hit me while I was still undoing the ribbon, but I carried on even though I knew before the paper fell open and the kids went hysterical that it was dog poo.

I pretended I wasn't hurt.

Mr Tristos pretended to explode with rage.

'Whoever brought this into class,' he yelled, 'will be punished,' but I could see his heart wasn't in it.

If he'd really wanted to punish someone he'd have kept the poo as evidence instead of taking it outside and chucking it in the bin.

In a town where the dogs are as friendly as this one, dog poo can be identified pretty easily.

I only got to look at it for a few seconds before my eyes got hot and my vision went blurry, and even after that short time I had the suspects narrowed down to a shortlist of three.

It doesn't matter.

A party on a bus was a dopey idea.

I'm just grateful I've realised that now instead of on the excursion.

Because now I've got the chance to come up with a better plan.

Doug, help.

We're handing in our permission forms and when I turned just now to give mine to Mr Tristos, I saw them.

Troy and Brent Malley.

They're outside the window, staring at me.

Even their freckles are scowling.

What makes it worse is that their eyes are red.

37

Jeez, if the bank's made them cry I'm in deep poop.

Everyone knows the Malleys don't cry.

Perhaps it's just dust. Their Dad's ute hasn't got side windows.

Except if it is dust, why are they looking at the playground where we all have to go at lunchtime and then back at me and mouthing words that almost all look like they begin with the letter F?

I'm trying to give them a friendly smile.

It's not easy.

My mouth doesn't want to smile, it wants to shout 'help'.

Troy and Brent aren't smiling back.

They're swinging their school bags over their shoulders like they probably do with wild pigs they've shot or bashed up and now they're going down to their classroom.

I'm desperately trying to think what to do, Doug.

I could offer to find Mr and Mrs Malley other work, but I don't think that'd calm Troy and Brent down.

Not even if I offer to write to Hollywood and see if they can fit Mr and Mrs Malley into their next movie as hired guns.

I hope you're receiving this, Doug, and I hope you're not busy in seventeen minutes.

That's when the lunch bell goes.

The lunch bell's just gone, Doug.

I've squeezed my brain into turnip mash trying to work out how you can save me.

All I've come up with is you appearing in the playground and dazzling Troy and Brent with flying tricks and possibly some juggling.

Which shows how panicked I am.

I know perfectly well you're invisible so you won't show up on air traffic controllers' radar screens and so your work won't be hindered by adoring crowds trying to mob you.

Hang on, what's this?

A Year Two kid sticking her head round the door and yelling that Mrs Stegnjaaic in the office wants to see me.

You're a genius, Doug.

I wouldn't have thought of something as brilliantly simple as that in a million years.

How do you come up with stuff like that?

Do angels have to study and take exams, or

is it just a skill that develops naturally like pig shooting?

Either way, it's working.

If I keep my head down and keep on walking fast, in fifteen seconds I'll be in the office and Troy and Brent'll be scratching their heads in the playground thinking I've turned invisible.

Don't stop what you're doing, Doug.

If you're in the middle of something important like finding a kid lost in the desert without a hat, ignore me.

But if you can spare half an ear, you might be interested to hear how things went in the office.

Just like you planned, that's how.

Usually people are only called to the office for family emergencies, so I was half expecting Mrs Stegnjaaic to say something like 'your mum and dad are being held captive in the bank by a gang of armed farmers' or 'your gran accidentally set fire to a plate of chocolate crackles and burnt the house down'.

I was quite surprised when all she did was hold up my excursion permission form and say 'we need more information'.

For a sec I thought she meant more information about the excursion.

I wouldn't have put that past you Doug,

getting me away from the Malleys by having Mrs Stegnjaaic send me on a special three-day trip over to the coast to find out if the school there's got lockers.

Then I realised she meant more information about the name I'd put on the form under Next of Kin.

Your name, Doug.

I hope you don't mind.

'This isn't your dad's name,' said Mrs Stegnjaaic.

My heart started going a bit wobbly.

I explained that Mum and Dad have got a lot on their plate at the moment.

Mrs Stegnjaaic looked sympathetic. She can be really kind and understanding, not like Ms Dorrit the principal.

'Doug's not enough,' said Mrs Stegnjaaic. 'We need a full name and phone number.'

'Um,' I said, 'that's a bit difficult.'

At that moment Ms Dorrit came out of her office.

'Are you being a pest species again, Mitch Webber?' she said.

I shook my head and Mrs Stegnjaaic said I wasn't and explained the situation.

'So what's the problem?' said Ms Dorrit, turning back to me. 'Why can't you give us this Doug's full name, address and phone number?'

I told her I don't know what they are.

Ms Dorrit's eyes narrowed, which happens when she thinks kids are having a lend of her.

'Who exactly is this person?' she said in a voice that made my neck prickle.

I tried to swallow but my throat felt even more drought-struck than the district.

'A close friend,' I said.

Ms Dorrit's eyes narrowed so much I started worrying that if she tried to leave the room she'd walk into the filing cabinet.

'Perhaps,' she said, in a voice that grated almost as much as the gearbox on the council water truck, 'he could pop in and give us the information himself.'

I felt sick.

Ms Dorrit's eyes were stabbing into me.

'It's a bit tricky,' I said. 'He's invisible.'

Ms Dorrit took a deep breath.

She looked at me for ages.

'In other words,' she said, 'he doesn't exist.'

I couldn't help it, Doug.

I had to say it.

'Yes he does,' I said. 'He's my guardian angel.'

Ms Dorrit looked like she'd just swallowed a filling.

I explained to her how angels can't hang around all day because they've got other kids to protect and how you're squeezing me into your schedule as it is.

'Wouldn't be fair on the other kids to drag him back,' I said, 'just for paperwork.'

There was a snigger from the doorway.

We all turned.

Gavin Sims was standing there smirking.

Ms Dorrit told him to wait outside.

Then she turned back to me.

'Alright Mitch Webber,' she said in her death voice, 'enough of this nonsense. For wasting our time you can stand here, outside my office, silently, for the rest of lunch.'

I know I'm a dope, Doug, but for a fleeting second I panicked.

The awful thought hit me that perhaps you'd had to dash off somewhere so fast you hadn't had time to come up with anything to protect me after all.

Mrs Stegnjaaic gave me a sympathetic look and went back to her typing.

Then I saw Troy and Brent Malley staring at me through the window, their faces bulging with frustration.

Which turned to fear when Ms Dorrit went out and yelled at them and sent them away from the window.

That's when I realised I'm not being looked after by just any old angel, I'm being looked after by the top angel in the whole world, possibly the universe.

Getting me kept in for the whole of lunch

is one of the best things anyone's ever done for me.

Thanks, Doug.

Class has only just started after lunch and Mr Tristos has yelled at me already.

For daydreaming.

He was wrong.

I wasn't daydreaming.

I was coming up with another plan.

Doug, when you're keeping an eye on Dad at the Malleys' place this arvo, don't worry about Troy and Brent bashing me up.

I want them to.

It's OK, I haven't gone mental.

I reckon the kids at this school aren't as mean as they make out.

I reckon underneath they've got pretty good hearts.

And when they see Troy and Brent pounding me into dingo bait, I reckon they're gunna feel pretty sorry for me and realise this drought's tough on me and my family too.

OK, perhaps not dingo bait exactly.

Perhaps just a few cuts and bruises, Doug, and possibly a black eye as long as there's no loss of vision.

There's a frog that can live under the ground for nine years without coming up once to stretch its legs or have a pee.

We're doing it in class now.

When a drought starts it burrows down into the desert and stays there till things improve.

I wish I could do the same, Doug.

Not cause I'm scared.

Cause I'm ashamed.

Ashamed of my class and my teacher.

I reckon Mr Tristos must have damaged his hearing at the staff karaoke night.

When twenty-seven kids spend a whole afternoon making rude and insulting jokes about a person's guardian angel and the teacher doesn't hear any of them, that teacher should be thinking about major ear surgery.

Please accept my apologies, Doug, for my very rude class and a teacher who's obviously scared of doctors.

I know who told everyone.

Gavin Sims.

I reckon that's crook, eavesdropping on a private conversation between a person and a principal and then blabbing about it.

I'm turning round now and giving him the look you give ex-friends who've betrayed you.

He's smirking, but I bet he's tortured with guilt inside.

The other kids are still whispering and laughing.

I'm going to ignore them.

And I will, just as soon as Matthew Conn stops singing that dumb song about fairies.

This is only a thought, Doug, because you're the expert, but I reckon he'd shut up pretty quick if he found he'd accidentally stapled his tongue to the desk.

OK Doug, I know I shouldn't have had that thought about Matthew Conn's tongue.

It was too cruel, plus he doesn't have a stapler.

I'm glad you didn't do anything to him, or any of the others.

That means you're ignoring them just like I am.

Which is what they deserve.

It'd be tragic if their mean and vicious behaviour distracted you from doing any medical miracles or freeing any kids from terrorists' hideouts.

Or protecting Dad in a few minutes.

That's why I'm glad you're not letting yourself be distracted at the moment while Mr Tristos is out taking a phone call and Danielle Wicks is standing on my desk flapping her arms.

I reckon she's only doing it to impress Carla Fiami.

Carla's ignoring her, like me.

OK, I have got a few tears in my eyes, but that's normal when you're in a hated family.

No big deal.

Except I am having second thoughts about letting the Malleys bash me up.

I don't reckon these kids are capable of feeling sorry for a person.

Not unless that person's got internal injuries and an ear ripped off, and I'm just not prepared to go that far.

Don't worry Doug, I've worked out how to make it home without Troy and Brent Malley getting me.

I've just remembered a very wise thing Gran once told me.

'Tough kids,' she said, 'usually can't run as fast as scared kids.'

She's right, as long as the scared kids get a decent start.

As soon as the bell went I was out of my seat, out of the room and first to the pegs.

But even as I was grabbing my bag I heard someone come up behind me.

My heart started thumping louder than a water pipe when the tank's empty.

I turned round.

It wasn't Troy Malley.

Or Brent.

It was Carla Fiami.

My heart kept thumping.

Carla Fiami may not be as tough as the Malleys but she's almost as vicious.

And she does most of it with words.

'Bit slack, this dopey guardian angel of yours, eh?' she said.

Carla's got very black eyes with curly hair hanging over them and they glint in a way that makes most people really nervous.

I thought of explaining that you're not slack, Doug, just busy, but I didn't.

I reckoned she was just filling in time till the Malleys arrived so she could make sarcastic comments about their punching technique while they pounded me into sheep pellets.

Instead she grabbed me and said 'Come on' and dragged me outside.

I wanted to sprint for the gate, but it was too late.

Kids were coming out of all the other classrooms, including Troy and Brent's.

Carla dragged me round the back of the school hall.

'Climb up,' she said.

I stared at her.

The only way up was the drainpipe, but it collapsed ages ago when Paul Keighley's big brother tried to climb it and it's been leaning against the wall ever since.

Carla pushed it to one side.

Behind it, hanging from the gutter bracket, was a rope.

'Climb up and lie on the roof till they've gone,' said Carla. 'I did it last week when Ms Dorrit was after me. Or are you scared of heights?'

I opened my mouth to tell her that one of my ancestors could do backward dives off the high board at the town pool, then decided it wasn't a good time.

I started climbing the rope.

Carla gave me a push up.

'Guardian angel,' she snorted. 'You must be a complete dope.'

It wasn't a good time for an argument either, but I had to say something.

'No I'm not,' I said.

'Dreamland,' she said. 'Get real.'

'What makes you the expert?' I said.

'I had a guardian angel for seven years,' she said, 'then he dumped me.'

I almost fell off the rope.

I opened my mouth to ask her at least fifty questions but she told me to save my breath for climbing.

After nearly bursting both lungs and a kneecap, I finally got up here on the roof and stared down at her.

'Why?' I panted.

She didn't get my drift.

I meant why did her guardian angel dump her, but Carla thought I meant why was she helping me.

''Cause you invited me to your party,' she said. 'I couldn't come cause I was busy, plus I wouldn't be seen dead at your place, but thanks.'

Before I could say anything she ran off.

I can't stop thinking about what she said.

Even though I'm lying on scorching tin and I can hear Troy and Brent Malley looking for me down below, I can't keep my mind off it.

Dumped by an angel.

That's tragic.

She must have done something really bad.

Doug, when you've finished keeping an eye on Dad, could you get in touch with Carla's ex-angel and have a quick word with him or her and explain that even though Carla's got a hurtful tongue and a mean way of looking at people she's actually a pretty nice person inside.

Thanks, Doug.

I won't interrupt again.

I was wrong, Doug, I'm interrupting again.

Troy and Brent Malley have found the rope.

I can hear them climbing.

They'll be up here on the roof in about ten seconds.

I haven't got a knife to cut the rope.

It'll take me at least half an hour to bite through it.

I dunno what to do.

If I jump I'll be history.

If they get their hands on me I'll be dingo bait.

Doug, help.

That's better.

I'm not seeing double any more and my nose has stopped bleeding.

Once my knee stops swelling and the headache goes, I'll be pretty right.

I'm a lucky bloke.

Lucky to have you, Doug.

Without you I could have been really injured.

I'm also lucky the school hall's got high windows.

And that the teacher who had gym this arvo left the gym mats piled up.

Jeez, it was close but.

When I finally got a window open wide enough to climb through, Brent Malley was so near I could hear the saliva flapping in his windpipe.

If I hadn't jumped when I did, he'd have got a firmer grip on my leg and I'd never have been able to shake him off.

As it was he knocked me off balance, which is why I jumped head first.

And why I did the double somersault on the way down.

I just wish I could have done two and a half, cause then I'd have landed on my feet instead of my face.

Boy, high dives are faster in real life than on telly. I barely had a chance to yell before it was all over.

I can see why championship divers prefer water to gym mats. If they dived onto gym mats they'd spend half their lives staggering around in a daze dropping their trophies.

And if they ever had to sprint out of a school hall directly afterwards and run for their lives from the Malleys, they'd have real trouble reaching their top speed.

I am.

Thanks Doug, for looking after Dad.

He's just driven past without any visible bullet holes in him or the four-wheel drive.

Jeez, I'm relieved.

I waved and yelled, but he didn't see me.

I wish he had.

I don't know if I can run all the way home with this knee.

Plus I want to tell him about my dive.

I reckon he'd be really proud.

53

Even Grandad couldn't always do a double somersault.

Most of all I want to tell him about the Malleys' faces after I did it.

For a few secs, before they ran off to climb down and come after me, they stared down through the window.

And guess what, Doug?

They were impressed.

You should have seen their faces, they looked like ...

Oh, Doug.

I'm having an idea.

Keep my legs moving, Doug, please.

I can feel the blood rushing to my brain.

I think this is the one.

Yes.

Yes.

Yes.

Yes.

Why didn't I think of it before?

I'm gunna become a world champion diver.

Or at least an Australian one.

And when I've won loads of trophies and medals for diving off really high diving boards, and earned heaps of honour and glory for this town, the people round here'll have to feel differently about me.

And Dad.

People always like the dads of sports champions, it's a known fact.

OK, Doug, I know what you're probably thinking.

You're probably thinking I'm pretty dopey deciding to be a diver when there's not a pool, river, creek or dam in these parts with any water in it.

That's the whole point.

If I'm gunna impress people I've got to do something that no one else from this district can do.

I reckon I'm probably the only kid for six hundred thousand square kilometres around here who's planning to be a champion diver.

I've seen championship diving on telly and I know I can do it.

OK, not a triple reverse somersault with twist straight off, but I've already done a double forward somersault, and I reckon I could have added a twist if the Malleys hadn't rushed me.

After all, I've got diving in my blood.

And you to stop me having any tragic accidents, Doug.

If I can teach myself a triple reverse somersault by next week when we go on the swimming carnival excursion, I reckon I can win the diving over there and be off and running on the road to international success.

This is it.

The plan I've been looking for.

Jeez, I'm so excited my legs are going all wobbly.

I can hardly run any more.

I can't see the Malleys, but they can't be far behind.

Quick, Doug, I need a hiding place.

For a sec just then I thought Mr Bullock was gunna chuck me out.

He doesn't like kids hanging round his shop if they're not renting a video.

Thanks, Doug, for making Sheena's dog recognise me and lick me so much that Mr Bullock changed his mind and let me stay.

And thanks for giving me the idea of coming here.

The Action and Horror section in the video store's a great place to hide.

For a start, if I crouch down by this bottom shelf pretending to look for forgotten musicals Arnold Schwarzenegger made before he was a star, I can't be seen from the street.

Plus if anyone comes in they'll most likely go to the Water section rather than this one. Mr Bullock keeps movies with water in them in their own section at the front. *Twenty Thousand Leagues Under the Sea*, *The River Wild*, *A Fish Called Wanda*, that sort of stuff. They're the most popular type of videos round here since the drought started.

I must check out the ones with diving in them.

Troy and Brent Malley hate water movies.

All their favourite videos are in Action and Horror.

Everyone knows that.

Troy and Brent would never expect anyone they were after to hide in their section, not in a million years.

Good on you, Doug.

They'll never find me here.

Don't blame yourself, Doug.

It was a fluke, them finding me there.

I reckon they'd given up looking for me and had decided to rent a video with lots of killing in it to make themselves feel better.

Thanks for distracting them so I could duck past them and run for it.

That was a top move, having Mr Bullock call them over to the counter to pick up that copy of *Death on the Nile* their parents had reserved.

With that sort of start I've got a good chance of getting home before they catch me.

As long as I don't stop running.

~

You probably think I was pretty dopey to stop running, Doug.

Perhaps I was.

But it was something I had to do.

Halfway down our street I had a sudden vision of me spending the rest of my life being chased by Troy and Brent Malley and never having a chance to do any diving.

People just don't get to be international diving champs if they're always being knocked off balance by angry twins, it's a known fact.

So I decided to face up to them and get it over with.

The problem was, once I'd stopped and turned round and Troy and Brent had stopped and got over their surprise, everything happened too fast.

Before I could catch my breath and tell them I'd fight them one at a time, they were both on me and Troy was pushing my face in the dirt and kneeing me in the back and Brent was kicking me in the side and giving me Chinese burns on both arms at once.

I know you'd have saved me, Doug, if I'd called.

I still don't know why I didn't.

The Chinese burns must have affected my brain.

All I could think of was a completely dopey idea.

That Dad would save me.

I must have been delirious.

Dad isn't that sort of person. He's tried to rescue me a few times, for example the time I accidentally shut myself in the safe at the bank, but he panics and knocks things over and other people have to do it.

Just now but, when Troy and Brent finally stopped thumping me and I realised it was because someone had chucked cold water over us, for a sec I really thought it was Dad.

Yes, I thought, at last he's finally made his arms and legs do what he wants in a time of crisis.

But when I blinked the water out of my eyes it wasn't Dad standing there with a dripping bucket, it was Gran.

I still can't believe it.

Gran can get pretty angry, specially when Mum and Dad try to make her give up smoking or throw Grandad's overalls away, but I've never seen her as ropeable as she was just now.

Her eyes were like glowing cigarette tips, and even though she was wearing her saggy dress, the way she stuck her chest out made her look even taller than usual.

'You two mongrels on your feet,' she yelled at Troy and Brent.

They scrambled off me.

'If you want to bash someone for chucking you off your land,' Gran said to them, 'go in there and bash his dad.'

She pointed to our place.

Troy and Brent stared at her.

I stood up quickly in case they accepted her offer, but they didn't.

'Otherwise take a hike,' said Gran, 'and if you go crooked on this bloke again instead of those that deserve it, I'll tear strips off you wide enough to ...'

Gran stopped for a cough.

Troy and Brent didn't hang around for her to start yelling again.

They wiped the muddy water off their faces and glared at me and ran.

'You OK?' asked Gran when she'd finished having a spit.

I nodded.

My back was aching and my side was throbbing and my arms were burning but I hardly noticed any of it.

I was too busy noticing the look on Gran's face.

I know you made her come and rescue me, Doug, and I'm really grateful.

But seeing her peering at me like that, her face all pink and concerned, I had the weird thought that even if you hadn't made her rush out with that bucket of water, she probably would have anyway.

Mum went gastric.

'Oh Jeez!' she yelled. 'Ring Doctor Masterton.'

Mum, I thought, stop over-reacting.

Then I remembered that as well as being dripping wet and covered in dust and a bit scraped around the chin, I still had blood on my nose and a swollen knee from the gym mats.

'It's OK, Mum,' I said, 'it'll wash off.'

Sonya Masterton reckons her dad's work-load has doubled since the bank started chucking people off their farms and I didn't want him taking it out on me with tetanus injections.

'Where's that hopeless husband of yours?' said Gran to Mum, grabbing me by the shoulder. 'I want him to take a squiz at this. See what his precious bank's doing.'

My side started throbbing harder.

'No,' said Mum. 'Noel's had enough today. Head office just rang. Mr Grimmond reckons Noel's reports are too soft. Told him he's making too many excuses for the farmers. Told him to get tougher or else. He's taken a Panadol and gone to bed.'

Poor old Dad.

He's probably feeling as bad as I am.

I'm in the bath now, checking out the damage.

Few bruises mostly.

Nothing that'll get in the way of diving practice.

What I need is some softer gym mats.

Gran's just been in.

I wish she'd knock.

She might be good at handling bullies but she's got hopeless manners when it comes to bathrooms.

She told me to run more water and soak my bruises properly, but I didn't cause we're getting low and the next delivery's not for ages.

Plus she's already used a bucketful out in the street.

'Thanks, Gran,' I said. 'You really put the wind up the Malleys.'

Gran waved a letter at me.

'I wouldn't have done it,' she said, 'if I'd known you'd been stealing my mail.'

I stared up at her.

'It was in your school bag,' she said. 'Dunno how a person's meant to manage their investments when letters from their bank get left in school bags.'

I realised what had happened.

This morning, when I was at the mail box checking for birthday cards and I panicked about Dad and the Malleys, I must have stuffed her letter in my bag.

'Sorry, Gran,' I said.

She grunted.

I saw her looking at my bruises and I could tell she was blaming Dad.

'It was my fault,' I said. 'I wanted to fight the Malleys and get it out the way so I can concentrate on being a champion diver.'

She stared down at me.

'I knew I wouldn't get too bashed,' I said, 'cause Doug's back looking after me.'

Gran's stare turned into a frown.

I hope I didn't hurt her feelings, letting her know she didn't save me single-handed.

I hope she was just frowning cause Grandad's been dead seven years and it's a long time since she's seen a willy.

G'day Doug.

If you've got a sec, I'll explain what I'm doing up here on the roof.

And what all the mattresses and pillows and cushions from the house are doing piled up down there on the ground.

It's like this.

Last night before I went to sleep I decided to get a bit of diving practice in.

Mr Tristos is always saying that to learn something new you've got to do it several times.

Trouble is, it's really hard doing a double somersault off the top of a wardrobe onto a bed.

The most I could do was a single somersault with a half twist.

I hadn't even planned the half twist, I had to do it to avoid the bedside lamp.

For a double somersault you need extra height, so now Mum and Dad have left early for work, I've decided to use our roof.

The reason I'm telling you all this, Doug, is I'm a bit worried that if I bounce off the mattresses at the wrong angle there might not be enough pillows and cushions to stop me splitting my skull open and scattering teeth all over the driveway.

I don't want to wake Gran up to ask her for her pillow, so I'm asking you to keep an eye on me.

Thanks, Doug.

OK, I'd better stop yakking and get a few dives in before my soles melt and stick to the roof.

I don't want to be up here scraping my thongs off the tin when Gran wakes up.

If Mum and Dad find out about this they'll go mental.

Mum and Dad have gone mental.

I've tried to explain to them it's partly their fault for coming home only ten minutes after they left.

They should have told me they were just going to Conkey's for tights and aftershave.

But they won't listen.

They're too busy yelling things up at me like 'don't move' and 'step back off the guttering' and 'I'm gunna tan your hide' and 'don't jump, we love you'.

I'm trying to tell them about my diving

career and how I was never in serious danger and neither were the lounge room cushions because you were protecting me, Doug.

I know they don't believe in you, but I don't know what else to say.

I've got to calm them down somehow.

Oh, no.

Dad's climbing up the ladder.

Help him, Doug, please.

No, it's OK, I can handle it.

Once I've unhooked his trouser leg from the TV satellite dish and unjammed his shoe from the bathroom window, he'll be fine.

Doug, are you feeling hurt?

You know, by the things Mum and Dad have just been saying about you?

They weren't really about you.

When Dad said 'Oh God, not again', it was mostly because when I got him off the ladder he was so tense he sat on the four-wheel drive winch and ripped his daks for the second time this week.

When Mum said 'Mitch, I thought we agreed three years ago you were too old for all this invisible friend nonsense', she only used the word nonsense because she was tired and stressed and wondering how she could get two windows fixed before work.

When Dad said to Mum 'It's all your

67

mother's fault for filling his head with loony hairbrained gibberish in the first place', he was just letting off steam because of the unkind things Gran says to him, and possibly because the winch had irritated his upper thighs.

I hope that makes you feel better, Doug.

Now we're all sitting at the breakfast table and there's some silence at last, I'm gunna try and work it out.

The thing that's puzzling me.

Doug, why didn't you delay Mum and Dad a bit?

To give me time to get at least one dive in?

After they left Conkey's you could have made them drop into the Gas 'N' Gobble for some touch-up paint to cover the rude words people have scratched on the side of Dad's four-wheel drive.

You could have inspired them to come home via the scenic route past the abattoir.

Why didn't you, Doug?

Was it cause you're angry with me for having parents who don't believe in you?

Hang on a sec, Mum's just started to cry.

'You could have been killed,' she's saying.

Poor thing.

I feel terrible.

I wish I could make her feel better.

All I can do is hug her.

'For God's sake speak to him,' she's saying to Dad.

We're all waiting.

Dad looks pretty upset too.

'You could have been killed,' he's saying.

He's just knocked the milk over.

'Hopeless,' Gran's saying.

Everyone's silent again.

I reckon I know the answer, Doug.

I reckon you're not angry.

Mum and Dad can't help what they believe, you know that.

I reckon you stopped me diving this morning for their sake.

In a town this small, they'd find out sooner or later about me diving onto gym mats and lounge cushions, and the stress would be too much.

Look at poor old Dad.

He's so stressed he's just shut his tie in the fridge.

Now he's glaring at the fridge door like he's planning to write a report on it.

OK, Doug, I get the message.

From now on I'll only dive into water.

I just wish the excursion was tomorrow instead of next week.

When the bus gets to the coast, I'm gunna spend half a minute having a squiz at the sea, just to check out what it looks like, then

I'll go straight to the pool and start practising.

Doug, please make Dad's heart valves stand the stress until the excursion.

The excursion's been cancelled.

Ms Dorrit just told us in assembly.

Kids are almost in tears.

Me included.

Leaving the hall we were all numb, just sort of staring at the ground.

Well, I was staring at the ground.

The others were staring at me and muttering how it was all my fault.

Luckily I didn't have to go into class with them. Ms Dorrit sent me to stand here outside her door after what she reckoned was my outburst in assembly.

I reckon an outburst's only human with news that bad.

What got me was she didn't even look sad.

When a school principal stands up in assembly and comes out with news that crook, you'd think she'd at least look sad, eh Doug?

'I've got some very disappointing news,' she said after we'd finished singing.

71

I reckon she's not disappointed at all.

I reckon she's glad.

I reckon she never liked the idea of a school excursion in case Cathy Saxby chucked on the bus.

'Regretfully,' she said, 'we haven't had enough bookings for the excursion and I have no alternative but to cancel it.'

My insides did a dive.

No somersaults.

No twists.

Just a straight plummet.

I looked around.

I've never seen a hallful of kids so sad.

Most of the kids in this town can't even swim and that trip to the coast was their only chance to learn.

I could see what they were thinking.

Andy Howard was thinking that if he ever visits a Mexican food factory and falls into a vat of taco dip and finds he can't eat it fast enough, he'll drown.

Sheena Bullock was thinking that if she and her dog join the police force and chase smugglers and her dog gets hit on the head with a surfboard stuffed with jewels, she'll never be able to swim over and rescue him.

Danielle Wicks was thinking that when she becomes Prime Minister, if she falls into that lake in Canberra she'll be history.

Carla Fiami was looking sadder than any of them.

I reckon she was thinking about her childhood growing up on the coast and how she'll probably never get to have another swim ever again.

I knew what they were all thinking because I was thinking about my future life too.

Not a life of international sporting glory and having my picture taken with Dad for the bowls club newsletter.

A life of being hounded from town to town and only being spoken to by the kids of dentists and parking inspectors.

A life of brooding how close I'd come to saving my family.

And how I'd failed.

I looked up at Ms Dorrit on the stage.

'You can't,' I said.

She looked stunned, then glared down at me.

My mouth was dryer than a lawn sprinkler.

'You can't cancel the excursion,' I croaked. 'Do you have any idea what it's like to drown in taco dip?'

It was a pretty dumb thing to say, but it didn't matter because Ms Dorrit ignored it.

'I didn't choose this, Mitch Webber,' she said. 'It breaks my heart too.'

I didn't know I was gunna say the next thing till I'd said it.

'Bull,' I said to Ms Dorrit. 'If you really cared you'd get our pool here in town filled so the kids and dogs of this district could learn to swim and we could have our own swimming carnival.'

Ms Dorrit's eyes narrowed.

'And diving competition,' I said.

She opened her mouth.

For a sec I thought she was gunna say, 'Good idea Mitch, I'll order the water today.'

Instead she just pointed to her room.

As I walked out, she turned back to the assembly.

'It's not my choice,' she said. 'I've been contacted by many of your parents. They've told me they just don't have the money for an excursion, not with the drought on, not with all their other financial problems.'

As soon as she said that, every kid in the hall stopped looking at her and turned and looked at me.

Not just looked at me, glared at me.

Suddenly I couldn't breathe.

All around me, eyes were ripping into me like bullets.

Not just Troy and Brent Malley's, everyone's.

I've never seen a hallful of kids looking so mean.

If they'd had cattle trucks they'd have driven them over me there and then.

My guts did a slow belly flop as I realised what they were thinking.

I opened my mouth to try and explain, then gave it away.

I knew they'd still be thinking what they were thinking even if I explained for hours.

Even if I yelled till I was blue in the face.

The excursion's off, they were thinking, because of Mitch Webber's dad.

Oh well, thanks for making Ms Dorrit not expel me, Doug.

I know you couldn't do anything about the excursion.

An angel's job is to protect people, not fix up their travel arrangements or fill up their swimming pools.

Some problems can only be solved by us people ourselves.

That's why instead of going back to class I'm squeezing through this hole in the school fence.

Mayors should be more polite and considerate, that's what I reckon.

If a person comes into their video store for a meeting, they should turn the volume down on their TV.

How can anyone be expected to discuss serious council business with *The Little Mermaid* blaring in the background?

Mr Bullock couldn't even hear what I was saying at first.

'The swimming pool,' I shouted.

He turned the video down.

'I reckon,' I went on, 'if that pool was filled it could save this town. Truckies would stop off for a dip and spend money at the kiosk and tourists would come and pay fees at the camp-ground and the local economy would boom and the bank wouldn't have to chuck families off their properties and who knows, someone from round here could become an international diving champion and really put this town on the map.'

Mayors ought to be more dignified, too.

When someone suggests something really important to them they ought to look serious and say 'I'll make sure the council gives it their fullest consideration next time we're having a drink at the bowls club'.

Not laugh out loud and stick their hand down their shorts for a scratch.

When I'm world diving champ and I come home to accept the keys of the town, no way am I accepting them from him.

Anyway, he's wrong.

I'm absolutely positive that if the council bought half a million litres of water for the pool, people would not think it was the same as the councillors sticking the money in their bottoms, setting fire to it and doing cartwheels around town.

Mr Bullock's also wrong about the state of the pool.

I'm checking it out now and it's nowhere near as bad as he says.

OK, the fence is very rusty, but that's only a problem when you're climbing over it in a white T-shirt like I just did.

The turnstiles are pretty rusty too, but

they'll soon loosen up once kids start pushing them with blockout on their hands.

And the steps up to the diving board have seen better days, but people aren't idiots, they're capable of looking out for a few loose bits of concrete and a wobbly handrail.

Down here inside the pool itself things aren't too bad at all.

The paint on the bottom and sides is peeling a bit, but you've got to expect that when it's been dry as a duck's dunny for eight years.

The important thing is there are no big cracks, so it won't leak.

When these soft drink cans and chip wrappers and old shotgun cartridges are cleaned out it'll be good as new.

Once I've got it filled up.

Which won't be easy.

Gran always reckons when you've got a problem, make a list of all the things you could do to solve it, even the dopey ones.

Here goes.

I could ring the city and pretend to be the Gas 'N' Gobble and order two million cans of Coke and use them to fill the pool. Trouble is parents'd be dragging their kids out every five minutes to make them clean their teeth.

I could stick lots of hoses together and syphon the beer out of the bowls club. But then only people over eighteen would be allowed in the pool.

I could persuade everyone in town to come down here on a really hot day and sweat a lot. If I lived in a town with more people.

No Doug, it'll have to be water.

It'll be pretty hard getting hold of half a million litres of the stuff, but it's the only way.

It'll be pretty risky, too.

Not just for me, for the other kids as well.

Some of them might need an eye kept out for them.

I'll do the best I can Doug, but I might need some help, OK?

For a while it looked as if the meeting was going to be as big a disaster as my birthday party, even though I tried even harder this time.

I made the invitation sound as important as I could.

VERY IMPORTANT MEETING, I wrote. THIS MEETING COULD SAVE YOUR LIFE. IF YOU EVER PLAN TO VISIT A NON-DROUGHT AREA (EG CANBERRA, THE COAST OR A TACO DIP FACTORY), BE AT THIS MEETING. AFTER SCHOOL AT THE DUMP. NO PARENTS OR DOBBERS.

I stuck an invitation in every school locker like last time, but this time I included a map. Even though it wasn't really needed cause everyone in town goes to the dump at least once a week with their garbage, twice if they're looking for fridge parts.

When I got to the dump it was deserted.

Except, for a sec, I thought you were there Doug.

A breeze was making the plastic bags flap and was pinging the dust against the old tractor parts.

Then I remembered how Mr Conkey once explained that air movement at the dump is caused by gas from rotting potato peel. (At the time he was trying to get everyone to buy frozen potato wedges.)

I waited by the piles of plastic drink bottles we collected last year when the council went on a recycling craze. We saved bottles for months, right up until someone remembered the nearest recycling plant is two thousand kilometres away.

By ten past three only two kids had arrived and they ignored me and started chucking Mrs Nile's bedsprings at each other.

By three-fifteen I was desperate.

I started wondering if a diving competition could be held in real life with just wardrobes and beds.

Then I saw a bunch of about twenty kids coming towards me.

As they got closer, looking hot and annoyed, I saw Carla Fiami behind them, yapping at the stragglers' heels like a cattle dog.

'You'll never know if he's crapping on or not if you don't give him a listen,' I heard her saying to Troy and Brent Malley. 'Give him

81

five minutes and if you still reckon he's a slimebucket, bash him up then.'

Carla grinned at me and I gave her a grateful look, but not too grateful.

The kids gathered round and I climbed up onto Mr Saxby's old ute and tried to ignore Troy and Brent's noisy breathing.

'I've worked out a way,' I said as loudly as I could, which wasn't very loud cause my throat was dryer than a lawn sprinkler, 'of getting the pool filled.'

The kids stared at me.

The dump was silent except for the flapping plastic and the pinging dust and the sound of Emma Wilkinson getting her foot jammed in a paint tin.

'Bull,' said Troy Malley after a bit.

'You're gunna ask my uncle, right?' said Hazel Gillies. 'His tribe can get water out of rocks with wallaby guts. He'll fill the pool for youse. Next year when he gets back from Perth.'

I thanked Hazel for her offer and pointed across the dump at the reservoir tower in the distance.

'There's enough water in there to fill the pool,' I said. 'More than enough. Six hundred thousand litres.'

The kids stared at me even harder.

Carla was starting to look worried.

Troy and Brent Malley were starting to look impatient and angry.

'You can't use that,' said Matthew Conn. 'That's the town's water supply. That's got to last till the next delivery.'

'If you use that,' said Danielle Wicks, 'what are we meant to wash in?'

'What are we meant to drink?' said Sean Howe.

'What are we meant to boil two-minute noodles in?' said Andy Howard.

'The people round here need that water,' said Jacquie Chaplin.

'That's why,' I said, 'we're gunna let them use it first.'

During the silence that followed I jumped down from the ute and grabbed an armful of empty plastic drink bottles and started handing them round.

Most of the kids looked puzzled, specially Troy and Brent Malley.

Carla Fiami grinned.

Three bottles.

Not bad for one evening.

It would have been more if Mum had boiled something for dinner instead of microwaving, and if I'd been a bit quicker with the sponge when Dad dropped the kettle.

Tomorrow after school I'll get a proper plug for the shower.

I don't know if you've ever tried to save your shower water, Doug, but you're fighting a losing battle when the plug's made of toilet paper and keeps going soggy.

Come to think of it, angels probably don't need showers. You probably just fly so fast all the dirt gets blown off.

Thanks for keeping Gran out of the bathroom while I was getting the shower water into the bottles.

Best if the adults don't know about the plan yet.

If they knew there was a secret stash of water in town, they'd probably all want to wash their cars.

I think the plan's gunna work, Doug.

I just saw Carla in the playground and she's got six bottles already.

Six bottles in less than a day.

She explained that only two are from her place cause they've got a special shower spray that hardly lets any water through, plus she got shampoo in her eyes this morning and kicked the plug out and lost about another two bottles.

The other four bottles are from the Gas 'N' Gobble.

Carla had to meet her mum there yesterday after the meeting and Geoff the mechanic was flushing out a ute radiator and she asked if she could have the water.

She said it was for a project, which is almost true.

Pretty smart thinking, eh Doug?

Water's water, even if it is a bit rusty.

If all the kids are as on the ball as Carla, we'll have the pool filled in no time.

OK, not all the kids are as on the ball as Carla.

Just now going into class Danielle Wicks saw me and tried to walk the other way so I cornered her.

She showed me what she'd collected.

Half a bottle.

Half a bottle from a family of seven.

'What about all the people having showers at your place?' I asked.

'We don't get showers on Thursdays,' said Danielle, 'just a bath with all of us using the same water.'

I looked at her half bottle in amazement.

'Seven of you have a bath in that much water?' I said.

'Don't be a pin brain,' she said. 'We use heaps more than that but Ryan goes last and he lets the dogs drink it.'

I asked her to keep her voice down. We

were pretty close to the offices and Ms Dorrit's got ears like a council irrigation inspector.

Quietly I suggested to Danielle that the more she can stop their dogs running around and getting thirsty, the quicker we'll have the pool filled.

She scowled.

'Listen, smarty pants,' she said, 'don't get bossy just cause you can pinch crates of bank water. Your dad and his poxy bank are the reason our family's living in a poxy house in town in the first place with three dogs going mental in the yard.'

I decided not to get into an argument.

Life must be pretty tough for the Wicks's, plus when Danielle gets worked up her voice can be heard for miles.

I started to quietly explain to her that the bank doesn't supply its staff with water, just tea and coffee.

Danielle unscrewed her bottle and tried to tip it over my head.

With another 499,986 litres still to get we can't afford to waste water, so I shut up.

Most of the kids are trying to avoid me.

Andy Howard reckons trying to fill the pool is a dopey idea and that his mum's pot plants need the water more cause if her cherry tomatoes die she'll kill him.

~

Matthew Conn hasn't collected a drop.

He says his dad goes really crook if anyone in his family has a shower or washes clothes and doesn't use the water to top up the radiator in the truck.

I just bailed up Sean Howe in the boys' dunny.

He hasn't collected a drop either.

He reckons he doesn't dare cause his mum and dad use all their cooking water for making beer.

He offered to pee into a bottle, but I said no.

You'd think, wouldn't you Doug, that a townful of fairly intelligent kids could do a simple thing like save household water.

Jeez.

I can see why Mr Tristos gets so stressed when he has to try and organise everyone for sport. If I had a moustache like Mr Tristos I'd be chewing it right now, I can tell you.

I've just wasted three hours after school waiting for kids to turn up with some water.

OK, the time wasn't completely wasted. The first hour I spent clearing rubbish out of the pool changing rooms so we've got somewhere to stack the full bottles.

The next hour I spent finding the Stegnjaaics' old inflatable plastic swimming pool at the dump and dragging empty bottles back in it and hiding them in the pool kiosk.

But the last hour I just waited.

And did some thinking.

I reckon I know now what the problem is, Doug.

None of those kids believe in you.

None of them believe you can save them from being sprung by their parents and whacked round the head with wilting pot plants and dried-up home-brewing kits.

There must be something we can do to change that.

Sorry to disturb you so late, Doug, but I've thought of something.

I'm not sure if you're going to like it.

Or even if it's possible.

Oh well, here goes.

What I'm hoping, Doug, is that angels can stop being invisible for a bit and appear to kids.

You know, if there's a really really important reason for them to do it, like saving a town and a dad.

I've been thinking about it for hours since I went to bed and I reckon it is possible.

I read in the paper once about some kids in Peru who said they saw an angel, and I reckon they were telling the truth. I reckon Dad was wrong about them having fried their brains from sitting too close to their computer screens.

If their angel could appear to them, I reckon you could appear to a group of kids in this town standing on your head.

Not actually standing on your head but, though you can if you want.

In a blaze of light would be better.

With fireworks in the background.

And maybe some laser beams or something.

If I arrange things this end, could you do it tomorrow night?

Please?

It's all set, Doug.

Wasn't easy, but.

None of the kids believed me at first.

'Bull,' said Matthew Conn.

'As if,' said Jacquie Chaplin.

'Jeez, you're a pin brain,' said Danielle Wicks.

'It's true,' I said.

'Yeah, right,' sneered Andy Howard. 'What's this angel gunna do after he's appeared, drop into the Gas 'N' Gobble for some hot chips and a grease and oil change on his wings?'

The others all laughed, which just shows how desperate kids in this town are for real entertainment.

I frantically tried to think of something to take their minds off being pikers.

'It'll be pretty spectacular,' I said. 'Fireworks, probably.'

'I doubt it,' said Cathy Saxby. 'Seeing as there's been a total fire ban for the last eight years.'

'Pin brain,' said Danielle Wicks.

They started to wander off.

I was losing them.

Then Carla saved me.

'If Doug does show up,' she said, 'where's he gunna show up at?'

Her eyes were glittering and I couldn't tell if she was having a go at me or not.

Out of the corner of my eye I saw Troy and Brent Malley walking towards me across the playground with mean faces and that was when I had the idea.

'The Malleys' place,' I said loudly. 'Doug's gunna appear tonight down by the creek bed at the Malleys' place.'

The other kids stopped and turned and looked at Troy and Brent.

My mouth was dryer than a garden tap, but I made it keep on talking.

'And when the world hears about it,' I said to Troy and Brent, 'your place'll probably become a top tourist attraction and you won't have to move.'

Troy and Brent looked at each other.

Then they looked at me.

'Fair dinkum?' said Troy.

'Yes,' I said.

The other kids looked at me and then at Troy and Brent again and then at me again.

Brent put his face close to mine.

'If you're bulling, we'll do you,' he said.

'I know,' I said.

'What time?' asked Sean Howe.

I told them about eight.

Hope that's OK with you, Doug.

We're all here, Doug, and the other kids are getting a bit restless.

Troy and Brent reckon if you don't appear in the next minute they're gunna stab me.

It's too dark to see if they've got knives, but even if they haven't there's heaps of other things they could use out here in the scrub. Dry spinifex, for example. They'll find sharp bits easily, specially now the other kids are offering to help them look.

Carla's trying to calm them down.

She's telling them to go easy on me because I'm not a bad person, I'm just a bit of an idiot.

Sometimes I wish she wouldn't help quite so much.

I've already told them you're a bit late cause you're probably trying to decide what to wear.

Anything'll do, Doug.

Robes, a loincloth, overalls, anything.

And if the fireworks and lasers are holding things up, forget about them.

I've got a torch.

I did have a torch.

Troy and Brent have just taken it.

I think they're looking for a snake.

I think they're muttering something about my pants.

I can't hear exactly cause the other kids are sniggering too loudly.

Hurry, Doug, please.

Yes.

At last.

You're here.

Thank you.

The others have seen you too.

That's a great idea Doug, just having two beams of light instead of anything too flashy.

They look a bit like headlights coming towards us.

They are headlights.

Jeez, you're clever Doug.

Other angels would have floated down on a shimmering cloud with blinding special effects going off all over the place, but you've turned up in an ordinary old four-wheel drive so as not to scare anyone.

I can't believe it, Doug.

I've waited so long to meet you.

I'm so happy.

The tears are just cause your headlights are dazzling me a bit.

I'm over here.

The one waving.

You're waving too, I can see you now.

Leaning out of the driver's window.

Yelling.

Oh no, you're angry.

I must have dragged you away from something important.

Doug, I'm sorry, but now you're here you'll see that this is important too.

Look, the kids are all gawping.

Now they can see you with their own eyes they know they're being looked after by a real live top-quality guardian angel who'll keep them safe in even the riskiest water-bottling situations and . . .

Hang on a sec, Doug.

That's not you.

I know that voice.

I know that face.

I don't get it, Doug.

OK, I know you not turning up tonight must have been because you were flat out.

Guiding a school bus through a burning carwash, something like that.

And I know that not being able to answer my call would have probably made you feel pretty crook.

So sending someone else would have seemed like a good idea at the time.

But, Doug, why Dad?

I guess even angels don't always think straight when they're in the middle of a major rescue with blazing hoses and melting plastic buckets all around them.

If you'd had a moment to gather your thoughts you'd have realised that almost anyone would have been a better choice.

Mum.

Gran.

Mr Bullock with burning banknotes sticking out of his bum.

Anyone but Dad.

I've told you heaps of times how clumsy Dad gets when he's stressed.

One of the things that stresses him most is me being out in the bush at night.

He's got this thing about it ever since Marija Stegnjaaic got bitten by a scorpion at night and her tongue turned black.

This evening when Dad turned up at the Malleys' place he was so stressed he couldn't even drive properly.

He was crunching the gears so much he sounded like Gran eating chocolate crackles. That's why I thought it was you at first, Doug. Angels probably don't get much practice driving four-wheel drives.

The other kids weren't fooled.

They did stare at the four-wheel drive with their mouths open, but only after Dad had driven into a tree.

'Mitch,' he yelled after he'd checked for dents. 'Get in the vehicle.'

'That's not an angel,' said Sean Howe. 'That's your dad.'

'You're mental, Mitch Webber,' hissed Cathy Saxby. 'You should be living in sheltered accommodation.'

I got into the car, but only because I could

see Troy and Brent in the headlights running over to the house to tell Mr and Mrs Malley about their only tree.

Dad glared at me, then stuck his head out the window again.

'The rest of you stay here,' he yelled to the others. 'Your parents are on the way.'

The other kids looked at each other, then glared at me.

I couldn't hear what they were saying because Dad was revving the engine so much.

I didn't need to.

I'm getting pretty good at lip-reading swear words.

The four-wheel drive shot backwards.

And stopped.

Dad revved the engine even more.

'You can thank your lucky stars,' he shouted at me while he did it, 'that Ryan Wicks spilled the beans to his folks about tonight's little fiasco.'

Doug, I reckon that's really low.

Was that the only way you could get Dad out to the Malleys' tonight, by using a little kid like Ryan?

When Danielle finds out he dobbed, she'll kill him.

It was low, but not as low as what happened when Dad finally stopped revving the engine and found we were bogged in sand.

'Give us a push,' he yelled to the other kids. 'Please.'

None of them moved.

And when their parents arrived, none of them helped either.

They just looked at me and Dad stuffing sticks under the wheels and turned away.

Some even sniggered.

Even Carla didn't help, but that was probably because she was depending on Danielle Wicks' parents for a lift and she didn't want to offend them.

'I tried to tell you,' she said as she walked past. 'Only dopes believe in guardian angels.'

She had to say that cause Danielle was with her.

Me and Dad were there for hours.

Mr and Mrs Malley threatened to have us arrested for trespassing and soil erosion.

Finally we got unbogged.

'That Fiami girl, she's right about guardian angels,' was all Dad said on the way home.

I didn't say anything.

Carla's right about a lot of stuff but she's not right about that.

She's not, is she Doug?

I can't sleep.

My eyes keep watering.

I've been telling myself it's the sand in my undies pricking me, but it's not.

It's what happened tonight.

First at the Malleys' and then just now.

I heard Gran get up and go out to the kitchen so I got up too and went out for a chat.

'Want a chocolate crackle?' asked Gran.

She gets pains in her legs at night and chocolate helps.

I shook my head.

'Gran,' I said, 'am I too old to have a guardian angel?'

Gran looked at me and took a big puff of her cigarette.

I felt myself flinch, and it wasn't because I was scared she'd cough chocolate crackle over me.

It was because I was scared of what her answer would be.

She blew the smoke out and then did something she hasn't done for ages.

Came over and gave me a hug.

'Jeez Mitch,' she said quietly, 'if I'd known it was gunna go on this long I'd never have started it.'

I pulled away from her.

'What do you mean?' I said.

My chest felt all tight, and it wasn't because I'd strained it pushing the car.

Gran took another mouthful and another puff.

'When I told you that story about Doug,' she said, 'you weren't even knee-high to a tick.'

My chest suddenly felt like a water bag when people are squeezing it to get the last drops out.

'Story,' I said. 'What story?'

'You'd wake up bawling,' said Gran. 'When it rained. Used to do that in those days. You were only three and a bit but you had galvanised-iron lungs. Your mum was tuckered out and your dad was hopeless, so I used to come over and tell you a story. About Doug, your guardian angel.'

She reached over and gripped my arm.

Her fingers were really strong for a senior citizen.

'Mitch,' she said quietly, 'mate, it was just a story.'

I stared at her and waited for my mouth to stop twitching.

So I could tell her that she'd got it wrong.

That you're not a story, Doug, you're true.

She'd said so herself.

Night after night.

I clenched my teeth and pointed this out to her and started reminding her of some stuff.

How you saved me from the Malleys.

Twice.

Then I realised she couldn't hear a word over the coughing fit she was having.

I slapped her on the back and poured her a beer and I was just about to start again when Mum came in with half-open eyes moaning about the racket and sent us both back to bed.

'If you wake Dad,' she growled at me, 'after what you put him through earlier tonight, you're dingo bait.'

'Sorry,' I mumbled.

Gran grabbed me outside my room.

For a sec, Doug, I thought she was going to tell me she'd been pulling my leg and that you were as real as the yellow stains on her fingers.

She didn't.

She just gave me another hug, which was sweet of her even though it nearly dislocated my ear.

'We don't need angels, old mate,' she said. 'We can look after each other, eh?'

I looked at her crumpled ancient face and realised what's happened.

It's tragic, eh Doug, when old people start to lose their grip.

I should have spotted it earlier.

Gran's been putting her lipstick on wobbly for some time now.

Jeez, she gave me a scare, but.

Imagine if you were really just someone she'd made up?

If you didn't exist?

I'd be on my own.

Just me and dog poo for my birthday and a dad people won't help even when he's up to his axles.

Just thinking about it's making my eyes go drippy.

I hate it when brains do this.

Get flooded with scary thoughts late at night.

It's OK, Doug.

I know you do really exist.

That's why I'm just sniffling a bit.

If I was really on my own I'd be sobbing much harder than this.

My tears'd probably fill the town pool.

Yes!
Yes!
Yes!
Yes!
Yes!
Go Doug!
Yes!!!!!

I deserve to be tied down in the scrub with jam on my big toes and heaps of signposts so the ants can find me.

No, Doug, I do.

It's what I deserve.

For not having more faith in you.

For doubting the double-best guardian angel in the whole universe.

Give us a D!

Give us an O!

Give us a U!

Give us a G!

What does it spell?

GENIUS!

I dunno how you did it, Doug, but thanks.

If God ever retires, I reckon you should get the job, no argument.

When the shouting woke me up my heart nearly dived out of my chest.

We don't usually get big crowds in town that early on a Saturday, so for an awful sec I thought it was farmers with guns coming after Dad.

I think Dad did too.

When I came out of my room he was crouched behind the kitchen table.

Though that might just have been because he'd stubbed his toe on the fridge again.

'Don't worry, Dad,' I said, 'I'll check it out.'

I peered out the front door ready to duck bullets.

Then I realised the shouting wasn't angry and murderous, it was happy and excited.

When I got down to the main street, half the town was milling around.

There were plenty of farmers, and I could tell they'd just driven in fast because their dogs were still in the back of their utes. A dog won't go onto a bonnet till the engine's cooled a bit.

The farmers weren't loading guns and muttering things about Dad, they were yelling questions at each other and pointing out along the highway.

For a sec I thought it was you, Doug.

Making your appearance a bit late and in slightly the wrong place.

Which would have been fine.

Even geniuses with super powers beyond the reach of mere mortals can't be expected to read maps right every time.

When the cloud of dust everyone was pointing at got a bit closer and I saw it wasn't you, I wasn't too disappointed.

Not when I saw what it was.

'Jeez,' yelled a farmer next to me, 'look at the size of them.'

Actually, as road tankers go, I don't reckon they were that much bigger than the one that brings petrol to the Gas 'N' Gobble on the first Wednesday of each month.

They were shinier, that's all.

And they didn't have Shell written on the side.

Or black smears all over them like the one that delivers the council water. The one that everybody reckons used to carry road tar.

People just thought your tankers were bigger, Doug, because they were so gleaming and mysterious.

And there were three of them.

We don't get many mysteries in these parts.

Not ones that don't involve banks or governments.

That's why everyone ran along the main street next to your tankers yelling and hollering even before they knew where the tankers were going.

I knew where they were going.

That's why I yelled and hollered louder than anyone.

Because I was so happy.

When the tankers stopped at the pool and the first one backed up to the gate and the driver connected a huge hose to the rear, everyone else got pretty happy too.

Except Mr Bullock.

He must be the most depressed mayor in Australia, I reckon.

'You can't fill this pool without council permission,' he said to the driver.

The driver hesitated.

The rest of us ignored him and jumped into the pool and started clearing out the rubbish.

Mr Bullock knew he was beaten.

'Alright,' he said, 'but the council's not paying for this water.'

'It's taken care of,' said the driver.

For a heart-stopping sec I thought he was you, Doug.

He didn't have wings, but if crumb-trays on

106

toasters can be detachable, I don't see why wings can't be too.

Then Matthew Conn tried to turn the big tap at the back of the tanker and the driver gave him a slap on the head.

So I knew it wasn't you, Doug, cause you'd never hit a kid.

When the driver turned the tap and the jet of water hit the wall of the pool, I held my breath in case the tired old concrete exploded.

It didn't.

All that exploded was the loudest cheer I've ever heard in this town, including the day we got satellite TV and Mr Conkey sold Mars Bars at half price.

Mr Bullock had one last try for the title of Australia's Grumpiest Mayor.

'No swimming,' he yelled at a couple of kids who were about to jump in. 'Council health regulations. No swimming without pool chemicals in the water. It's unsanitary.'

When the drivers opened the storage compartments under the tankers and started dragging out the drums of pool chlorine, the cheer that went up was almost as loud as the first one.

Would have been louder, probably, if some of the farmers hadn't been using their energy to chuck Mr Bullock into the pool.

Thanks, Doug.

I'd hug you if I could.

I'm hugging my wardrobe and pretending it's you.

When I'm a champion diver I'll mention you in all my interviews.

Plus, when the pool opens for swimming this afternoon, I'm gunna tell everyone who provided the water.

They'll want to name the pool after you, no risk.

Have angels got second names?

Don't worry if you haven't, Doug.

You can use mine.

I hope you can see this, Doug.

The view from up here on this diving board is incredible.

I can see the whole town, and the abattoir, and the Gas 'N' Gobble who need to repaint their roof pretty soon, and every property Dad's ever dobbed on.

Well, almost every property.

I can't actually tell them apart cause they all look the same from up here.

Brown.

Sorry Doug, I'm forgetting you'd be used to panoramic views.

So I don't have to tell you how much smaller a swimming pool seems when you're looking down on it.

Specially when half the town's in it trying to learn how to swim.

There hasn't been this much splashing in these parts since Danielle Wicks' mum tried to wash six dogs in the one bath.

Nobody's drowned yet, so swimming can't be that hard.

I reckon once I'm in the water I'll grasp the basics pretty quickly.

With a bit of help from you, Doug.

I had lots of Rice Bubbles for breakfast, so at least I'll float.

That was a good thought, Doug, only half-filling the pool.

Sergeant Crean reckons the water's too shallow for diving into from up here, which has stopped everyone else from having a crack at being a world-champion diver.

Boy, it's a long way down.

It's OK, Doug, I'm not scared.

This isn't me trembling, it's just me shivering a bit in the breeze. We're not used to breezes around here.

Plus my blood's pounding a bit.

From excitement.

My first real dive.

I can't wait.

Well actually I can wait cause if I dive now I'll land on Mr Saxby.

And Mrs Saxby who's holding his neck brace while he practises butterfly.

And Gavin Sims who keeps sinking to the bottom cause he's using his dad's cricket bat as a kick-board.

And Jacquie Chaplin who can feel something uncomfortable in her swimmers.

And Hazel Gillies who's telling her it's Gavin's foot.

And ...

I know, Doug, I know.

I've got to wait for a patch of water and go for it.

It's the same as waiting for the right moment to tell everyone why they should put up a big sign saying DOUG WEBBER SWIMMING POOL.

While I'm waiting I'll just focus my mind.

That's the most important thing for a diver, focussing the mind.

All the telly commentators say so.

First I think arms.

Now I think legs.

Now I think what if Mr Saxby has a neck spasm and flops into my patch of water while I'm on my way down.

Now I think stop being such a worry wart.

Now I think Doug wouldn't let it happen.

Now I think he's already done something today that proves he's the most super-powerful and clever angel in the entire known stratosphere i.e. half-filled a pool in thirteen minutes without using a single plastic bottle.

Now I think if he can do that he can do anything.

Move mountains.

Move tired sheep.

End droughts.

Stop me flattening Mr Saxby or any member of his . . .

Hang on a sec.

Jeez.

Doug.

I'm so slow.

Of course.

You could.

After this morning I know you could.

Now I am trembling.

And not just cause Sergeant Crean's climbing up and yelling at me that the diving board's a prohibited area.

Don't worry about him, Doug.

Don't waste time giving him vertigo or leg cramps.

Listen to what I'm saying.

I'm going to ask you the most important thing I've ever asked you.

Ever.

Including when I begged you to save me from that killer spider in first year.

Doug, I'm asking you to end the drought.

Make it rain, Doug.

You can do it, I know.

It's just like what you did today only with more water.

Doug, ignore Sergeant Crean even though he is grabbing me a bit roughly.

Focus your mind, Doug.

End the drought.

Please.

Doug?

Are you there?

Ignore me if you've started focussing your mind on ending the drought, OK?

I know it's a huge job and the last thing you want is me yakking away at you. That's why I haven't been in touch for the last twenty minutes.

But if you haven't started yet, this is important.

I'm a bit worried you might be having problems.

You know, because weather's not really your department.

So I just want to say that if there is a heap of extra inter-departmental paperwork involved, I'll help you with it.

I can do really neat writing if I have to.

If Matthew Conn's not flicking dust balls at me.

So if you're bogged down with forms and

reports, get some of them to me somehow, OK?

Also, you might be having doubts about whether it's OK to change the weather pattern of an entire district just cause one kid asks you to.

Don't worry.

Everyone round here wants the drought to end.

They're desperate for it.

I'll give you an example.

When Sergeant Crean chucked me out of the pool just now I tried to explain why he had to let me back in.

'My guardian angel supplied the water,' I said, 'but he's busy now on an even bigger project so I've got to help him out and keep an eye on people and make sure they don't drown.'

Sergeant Crean wasn't convinced.

'Cathy Saxby's right,' he said. 'You are mental.'

He went back in.

I was about to follow him and tell him about my training programme and how once I've won lots of gold diving trophies it'll be his responsibility to guard them at our place and he'll probably get promoted to inspector.

Then something hit me on the back of the head.

I felt it splatter against the top of my neck

and when I looked down there were red bits on my shoulders.

It was a tomato.

I turned round.

Carla was standing there scowling at me.

'That's for Enid,' she said.

Or something like that.

It was a bit hard to understand because she had a can opener in her mouth.

Before I could ask her to speak more clearly she chucked another one.

'And this is for Roald.'

That's what it sounded like.

The tomato hit me in the chest.

Bits of it splashed up under my chin and the rest slid down my front.

I was numb with shock.

'Hang on,' I said. 'I don't even know these people.'

Carla glared at me through her curls and suddenly I realised why her eyes were glinting so much.

They had tears in them.

She took another tomato from the can she was holding and got ready to chuck it.

My T-shirt was sodden and I could feel tomato juice soaking into my swimmers. I hate canned tomatoes. That's the trouble with living in a drought-affected area, fresh vegies are so expensive.

I had to get the can away from Carla.

Before I could move, Carla's mum pulled up in their ute.

'Carla,' said Mrs Fiami sharply, 'get in the car and stop wasting food.'

Then she saw me.

Her eyes narrowed.

'Sorry,' she said to Carla, 'I thought you were wasting it. I didn't realise you were putting it to good use.'

Carla threw the whole can of tomatoes at me.

I ducked and they splattered against the side of the pool kiosk.

'That's for Paul, Judy, Gillian, R.L., Emily, A.A., Lewis, Anna and Louisa May,' shouted Carla tearfully.

I think those were the names.

I stared at her, desperately trying to think of a big family that had been chucked off their land lately.

'They're all gunna die,' yelled Carla, 'thanks to your dad.'

Mrs Fiami revved the ute and as they drove off I caught a glimpse of a big box of ammo in the back.

For a gut-churning sec I thought that Carla had persuaded a whole lot of her rellies to help the Malleys shoot Dad, then turn their guns on themselves.

Dopey, I know, but the shock I was feeling

must have been stopping the blood getting to my brain.

Then the blood must have started flowing again because I suddenly remembered something I'd heard about Carla.

How she gives names to all the sheep at her place.

Then I understood.

My guts stopped churning and just lay there, still and sad.

There's something farmers have to do in droughts, Doug, when they can't afford feed for their animals. It saves the animals suffering hunger and starvation.

No wonder Carla was so upset.

The Fiamis are going to shoot their sheep.

'Stop,' I yelled, running after the ute, 'you don't have to, the drought's gunna be over soon.'

They were too far away to hear.

That's why I'm hurrying out to their place.

To try and let them know.

I just wish their place wasn't so far away on foot.

Anyway, Doug, you can see how relieved they'll be when you end the drought.

If I can get there in time.

And even if I can't there are heaps of other families like them.

So if you're having doubts, don't.

As soon as I got to the Fiamis' fence, I saw them.

Sheep.

Skinny and dusty and not in a very good mood, but alive.

Yes, I thought, I'm in time.

And even though my feet hurt and my face was burning and I had dried tomato sludge on my neck, I jumped over the fence with a whoop of joy.

The sheep took a few steps back.

'G'day,' I said to the sheep.

They took a few more steps back.

Then a thought hit me.

What if these were only some of the sheep?

Sent over here so they wouldn't be mentally scarred by the awful violence taking place on the other side of the property.

'Is there an Enid here?' I asked.

The sheep looked at me blankly.

'How about Roald?'

No one put up their hoof.

'Paul?' I said, 'R.L.? Lousia May?'

The sheep nearest me did a poo and for a sec I thought she'd recognised the name, but she hadn't.

I listened carefully for distant gunfire, but all I could hear was my heart pounding.

I hurried over to the house.

Luckily it was quite close to the fence, only about two kilometres, so I was there in about fifteen minutes.

There didn't seem to be anybody around.

I still couldn't hear any gunfire, so I crept round to the back of the house hoping I wouldn't run into anything bad.

Like dead sheep.

Or Mrs Fiami pointing a gun at me.

Or Carla with a giant can of tomatoes.

I didn't run into any of those.

What I ran into made me stare and blink to make sure my eyes were working properly.

It was a boat.

The first boat I'd ever seen in real life apart from on telly.

I went over to it.

It was pretty big, longer than Dad's four-wheel drive probably, with yellow and blue paint that was peeling off and a cabin with a window and a windscreen wiper.

And it was propped up on bricks.

'Don't touch that!' yelled a voice.

Carla came out of the house scowling.

I was relieved to see she didn't have any vegetables with her.

'That's my Dad's,' she said. 'Get away from it.'

I got away from it and remembered why I was there.

'Have you done it yet?' I asked anxiously.

My mouth was drier than a garden hose.

'Done what?' said Carla.

'Shot the sheep,' I said.

Carla didn't blink behind her curls.

'We're waiting a couple of days,' she said. 'Mum's gunna plead with the bank one more time to lend us more money for sheep feed.'

'You don't have to,' I said. 'The drought'll be over any day. Doug's fixing it.'

Carla stared at me, still not blinking.

She seemed to be in shock.

I tried to help her snap out of it.

'So,' I said, 'want to come swimming?'

'I hate swimming,' she said.

I tried to think what to say next.

'Prefer sailing, eh?' I said weakly.

'I hate sailing,' she said.

We looked at each other.

'Plus,' she said, 'I hate bull.'

For a sec I didn't know what she meant.

'Angel bull,' she said with a scowl.

Don't take it personally, Doug, she was upset.

121

'Did you think angels were bull when you had one?' I asked her.

She had a think.

Her eyes went darker and glintier and I knew they were filling with tears.

'Not at first,' she said. 'Not till he dumped me.'

'Are you absolutely sure he dumped you?' I said. 'He might have just lost your address.'

Carla looked at me like I was something she'd found growing in her lunch box.

OK, it was a dopey idea.

I had a better one.

'Doug could get his secretary to make inquiries and find out what happened to him,' I said. 'What was his name?'

'Dad,' said Carla quietly.

I stared at her.

'And I know what happened to him,' she said. 'He fell off his fishing boat and drowned.'

She picked up a rock and hurled it at the boat.

'So don't waste my time with bull,' she said, picking up another rock and facing me. 'If you're gunna be a pin brain, rack off.'

I tried to think of something to say, something to make her feel better, but before I could Mrs Fiami stuck her head out of the house and glared at me.

I racked off.

I wasn't gunna bother you with this, Doug, you being so busy, but I've been thinking about it most of the way home and there's something I think you should know.

Remember I told you once about a dopey thought I'd had?

About Dad rescuing me?

Forget I ever thought it.

Poor old Carla thought her dad could be a guardian angel and look what happened.

I'm lucky, I've got the real thing.

I'll stick with you, Doug.

Sorry to interrupt again, Doug, but I just want to let you know things are looking pretty grim for Carla's sheep.

I decided to have a word to Dad about them.

It was almost dark when I got home and I thought Mum and Dad would chuck a fit.

Luckily they were doing paperwork so they weren't completely on the ball.

'Have a good splash, love?' said Mum, barely looking up. 'Get your new swimmers wet?'

I nodded and felt them sticking to my buttocks and hoped we weren't having tinned tomatoes for tea.

'Any clues yet,' said Dad, 'about who's behind the water?'

I opened my mouth to tell him, then closed it again.

One thing at a time, as we're always telling Gran.

'I reckon it was Martians,' said Gran without looking up from the telly.

'Kind-hearted lotto winner more like,' said Mum, 'touched by the way a group of misguided but determined young people had a punt.'

While Gran had a coughing fit and I banged her on the back, I explained to Dad about Carla's sheep and how if the bank lent Carla's mum more money they'd probably win an animal welfare award, plus get some good chops later on.

Dad gave a big sigh and rubbed his hand wearily over his face and knocked his paperclips over.

'I'm sorry, Mitch,' he said. 'I wish I could help, but the bank won't be lending Mrs Fiami any more money. She owes them a stack already.'

I pleaded with him.

Dad said he'd swing it if he could, but he knew he couldn't.

I saw the way his shoulders were slumped and I knew he couldn't as well.

'Hopeless,' muttered Gran.

'Don't worry,' I said, 'I'll ask Doug.'

Dad went out of the room.

Mum winced and rubbed her tummy.

I felt terrible I'd even mentioned it.

I should have known it'd be a waste of time.

I should have come straight to you, Doug.

Which is what I'm doing now.

Don't get me wrong, I'm not asking you to rush things.

As Gran always says, if you rush things you won't do a good job and you'll probably give yourself a stressed ligament.

On the other hand there are some sheep around here who are pretty desperate for a feed and a wash and who'll be getting a bullet instead if it doesn't rain very soon.

I can't sleep.

My body's tired, specially my feet and neck, but my brain won't knock off.

When I first went to bed I kept thinking I could hear rain, but the noises just turned out to be the fridge, then Gran making popcorn, then the wind blowing dust against the house, then Gran frying an egg.

Mum got up and made Gran go to bed, then came in to see if I was being kept awake by the wind noise.

Dust storms make people pretty nervous in these parts. As well as over-exciting livestock they make car engines go out of tune and play havoc with false teeth.

I told Mum not to worry, that you were keeping an eye on us, Doug.

I know that's not strictly true at the moment, but I don't want her to worry.

Mum gave a big sigh, of relief I suppose.

'Go to sleep, Mitch,' she said softly.

I wished she'd said it to my brain.

Immediately she'd gone it started thinking about Carla.

And her Dad.

And his boat.

And the bricks propping it up.

At first I reckoned it was just desperate for subjects to think about.

Then I remembered something that woke my guts up, and my lungs, and that bit of your chest that thumps when your heart beats fast.

The colour of the bricks.

Dirty pink with black bits.

Exactly the same colour, I suddenly remembered, as the brick that was hurled through our window.

And the same shape.

And the same size.

I tried to stop my brain thinking the next thought.

It wouldn't.

I had a vision of Carla chucking the brick.

I should feel angry, but I just feel like crying.

You'd feel like crying too, Doug, if you only had one friend and it turned out she'd chucked a brick at you and your family.

I've just taken a deep breath and told my

chest to go back to sleep and my brain to stop being so suspicious.

Heaps of people in the district have got dirty pink bricks with black bits.

The bush fire brigade hut's completely built of them.

So's Mr Howard the brigade captain's barbeque.

OK, they're all cemented down, but still.

Anyway, it could have been Carla's mum.

I'm making my brain think about something else now to cheer me up. How great it'll be when the drought's broken and Dad doesn't have to dob people any more and we can all become respected and well-liked members of the community.

I'm thinking about my birthday party next year.

Heaps of kids watching me do championship dives into the pool we'll probably install in the back yard.

Dad next to the fountain and the waterfall juggling ping-pong balls with his mouth.

Gran juggling chocolate crackles with hers.

It's gunna be great, eh Doug?

When I woke up and saw how late it was, I rushed out to the kitchen to gobble some Rice Bubbles so I could get down to the pool and do some dives before the water filled up with farmers.

Dad was at the kitchen table in purple undies.

I didn't know where to look.

I was glad Gran wasn't up.

She can be really cruel about Dad's underwear.

Don't be offended, Doug, if you wear purple undies.

I bet they look cool on you.

It's just that they look pretty tragic on over-weight Bank Liaison Officers.

I kept my eyes on the Rice Bubbles.

Then I remembered something.

Dad doesn't have any purple undies.

'Don't guts yourself,' said Dad, pointing to the big bowl I was filling. 'I'm not giving a diving lesson to a bloke who's gunna sink on me.'

I realised they were purple swimmers.

I stared at him in amazement, partly because I'd never seen him in swimmers before and partly because I couldn't believe what I'd just heard.

For a sec I thought being up on the diving board yesterday had damaged my eardrums.

It hadn't.

'I've been thinking about you fancying yourself as a diving champ,' said Dad. 'If a bloke from these parts wants to take on the world at that caper, I reckon he could use a few tips.'

I felt like doing cartwheels across the kitchen and hugging him.

Except there was something I had to ask first.

'Um ... Dad,' I said, 'do you know anything about diving?'

Dad grinned and hooked his thumbs into the waistband of his swimmers.

'I might be just a mild-mannered Bank Liaison Officer to you, digger,' he said, 'but I've been around and done a few things, OK?'

I reckon sometimes we have to trust people, eh Doug?

We're in the car on the way to the pool now, and I've just told Dad about you filling it.

130

He went quiet for a bit.

Then he changed the subject and explained why Rice Bubbles don't help you float, even if you eat them dry. It's got to do with digestive juices and compacting.

I'm glad he took the time to explain that.

I reckon if a person's good with the theory, there's a good chance he'll be OK with the practical stuff too.

The pool was just as crowded as yesterday.

All the Wicks's were there, climbing onto each other's shoulders and falling off with shrieks.

Not their dogs, but.

The whole pool was full of shouting, splashing people.

As me and Dad walked in, I wondered how Dad was gunna give me a diving lesson if there weren't any vacant patches of water.

I needn't have worried.

As soon as Dad stood at the edge of the pool and started showing me arm positions, the people in the water stopped splashing and shouting and started muttering to each other and backing away.

They're still doing it.

There's a patch of water in front of Dad big enough for an elephant to dive into.

Dad doesn't seem to have noticed.

He's probably concentrating on other things.

Like keeping his balance that close to the edge of the pool without falling in.

Oh, no.

He's fallen in.

Everyone's laughing.

People can be so predictable.

Just cause a person's been talking about the importance of keeping his arms and legs together and his neck and ankles straight, and then he's slipped and fallen into the water with his arms and legs and neck and ankles all over the place, people think it's funny.

Dad's very sensibly staying under water till the unkind laughter stops.

Jeez, he's got good lungs.

He's been under there for ages.

It's hard to see exactly where he is cause the water's pretty murky from the dust storm.

People are starting to look anxious.

I'm starting to feel anxious.

Dad's not that good at holding his breath, I've seen him try and do it after he's hit his thumb with a hammer.

Dad, where are you?

People are shouting and swimming towards where he disappeared into the water.

Doug, drop what you're doing, this is urgent.

Thanks, Doug.

Thanks for moving so fast.

Another second and I'd have jumped into the water and then I might never have found Dad with so many people swimming around yelling.

Making him float to the surface was a great idea.

It meant I could be the one to grab the back of his swimmers and drag him out.

It's much less embarrassing to be rescued by your own son than by a bunch of people who hate your guts, even if they do have to help with a bit of pushing.

I reckon Dad handled it really well.

After he'd finished coughing up pool water, he thanked everyone and pretended he didn't hear them muttering things like 'stay out of the water you cretin'.

I was proud of him.

Right up till we got to the car.

'Well,' he said, rubbing the bruise on his forehead where he'd banged it on the concrete on his way into the pool, 'not such a bad start, eh?'

I didn't know what to say.

Dad grinned.

'Next time,' he said, 'I'll leave my shoes on for better grip.'

I tried to smile.

'Few more lessons,' said Dad, punching me in the shoulder, 'and you'll be diving like a champ.'

I was trying to think of a way to tell him that we'd both be better off without the lessons when he put his arm round my shoulders.

'You and me,' he said.

I think I knew what he was gunna say next because my insides suddenly felt like they were doing a reverse double somersault off a thousand-metre cliff.

'We don't need any dopey old wizards, gremlins or angels,' he said, 'do we mate?'

Sorry, Doug, that's what he said.

I could hardly breathe.

I waited for my mouth to stop having spasms of indignation so I could tell him how not only did you just save his life, you're pretty close to saving the lives of six hundred sheep.

He didn't give me time.

'Mitch,' he said, 'I want you to stop filling your head with nonsense about this Doug character.'

'Sorry Dad,' I said, 'I can't do that.'

His arm dropped away from my shoulders.

'I'm not asking you,' he said. 'I'm telling you.'

I didn't say anything.

I was wondering whether angels are allowed to adopt kids.

'Well?' he said.

His face was going as dark as his bruise.

I could see it was pointless trying to argue.

I just shook my head.

'Jeez,' exploded Dad. 'Why won't anyone listen to me?'

He grabbed my shoulders and squeezed them hard.

'I forbid you,' he shouted, his face very close to mine, 'to talk about Doug, think about Doug, play with Doug, draw pictures of Doug, write letters to Doug, dream about Doug, invite Doug to your birthday party or have diving lessons with Doug.'

Then he got in the car and drove off.

It's the pressure, Doug.

The pressure of being the most hated man in town.

It's getting to him.

It's only natural.

My legs have almost stopped shaking.

When they have I'm gunna go home and talk to him.

I reckon he'll calm down when I remind him that if it wasn't for you, people would probably have just stood around this arvo and watched him drown.

When I got home, Mum and Gran were in the kitchen.

Mum went gastric.

'You can be a very selfish boy, Mitch,' she yelled.

Gran stood up for me.

Except because she's old she did it sitting down.

'Don't blame him,' she muttered through a mouthful of muesli.

'I am blaming him,' yelled Mum, 'because he knows the pressure Noel's under and he still carries on with these ridiculous fairy stories.'

Gran had a small coughing fit.

I think it was mostly guilt.

'Where is Dad?' I asked after I'd banged Gran on the back.

'He's taken a Panadol and gone to bed,' said Mum.

'Hopeless,' muttered Gran.

Mum gave a big sigh and pushed me down into a chair next to Gran.

'Mr Grimmond from the bank is coming up from the city day after tomorrow,' she said. 'Dad reckons Mr Grimmond's coming to give him the sack.'

The kitchen spun a bit.

I could see why Mum had sat me down.

Even Gran looked shocked.

'Why?' I managed to ask.

Mum sighed again.

'Dad wrote a report on the Fiami property,' she said. 'Mrs Fiami owes the bank a heap of money and she's going broke and can't pay them. Dad knew the bank'd take her farm if they found out so he left it out of the report.'

'Good on him,' said Gran.

I thought so too, but I was puzzled.

'Why did he do that for the Fiamis,' I asked, 'when he's never done it for anyone else?'

'He's done it a bit for other families,' said Mum, 'but he went further for Carla and her mum because he didn't want you to lose the only friend you've got.'

I stood up to go and give Dad a hug.

I'd been feeling numb since he disappeared into the water this arvo, but suddenly I just wanted to throw my arms round him.

Then a thought hit me.

'With all this on his plate,' I said, 'why did he try and give me a diving lesson today?'

Mum sat down and closed her eyes, but I

could still see tears squeezing out from under her lids.

'Because,' she whispered, 'he's your dad.'

That's when my own eyes started to get hot and drippy.

Mum pulled me onto her lap and put her arms round me and we sat like that until Gran lit a cigarette and inhaled a piece of muesli.

OK, Doug.

I know this is the point where you'd normally leap into action.

But this time I don't want you to.

You've had enough interruptions and it's more important you finish the drought job.

I'll take care of this bank bloke.

After Mum had gone to look after Dad, I asked Gran for a hand.

'It'd be a tragedy if Dad got the boot now,' I said, 'before the drought breaks. He'd be remembered forever as a mean and nasty person.'

Gran agreed.

'What we need to do,' I said, 'is get hold of Mr Grimmond between the airstrip and the bank and keep him somewhere till it rains.'

Gran stared at me.

'The roof of the school hall,' I suggested.

Gran coughed and spluttered so hard that muesli pinged off the microwave.

'That's kidnapping,' she said.

'OK,' I said desperately, 'we could bribe him.'

'What with?' said Gran. 'Empty soft drink bottles?'

I had an idea.

'Your savings,' I said. 'Dad'll pay you back once the drought's broken and the bank can afford to give him a raise.'

'Sorry,' said Gran. 'I'm skint.'

I knew why.

'Dumb cigarettes,' I said. 'They shouldn't make 'em so expensive.'

Gran looked hurt and took a deep wheezy breath.

She started to say something.

'It's OK, Gran,' I said gently. 'You don't have to make excuses. We'll kidnap him.'

Gran put her spoon down.

'In my experience,' she said, 'there's something that works better than bribery or kidnapping.'

I hoped she wasn't gunna say murder.

'Friendship,' she said.

I thought about it.

I thought about Carla and how good that was while it lasted.

I reckon Gran's right.

This is just to let you know, Doug, that everything's under control.

I won't be going to sleep tonight till I've

139

figured out how I can get to be such good
mates with Mr Grimmond that he'll keep Dad
in the job and give him extra money to lend
Mrs Fiami to keep her going till you've ended
the drought.

Just a quick update, Doug.

I was awake most of last night, but I couldn't crack it.

The idea didn't come to me till this morning at school.

Even then I was so tired I almost missed it.

Ms Dorrit made the announcement in assembly and it just rolled over me like mineral water off a duck's back.

Then all the other kids started cheering and yakking to each other excitedly.

'Swimming carnival!' they were saying. 'We're having a swimming carnival!'

Suddenly I was listening so hard I could hear the sheets of paper rustling in Ms Dorrit's manila folder.

'... very fortunate,' she was saying. 'The council were going to close the pool from today on account of the filter being clogged by Saturday night's dust storm. However they've agreed to leave it open one more day so tomorrow we can have our first school swimming carnival for eight years.'

Everyone cheered again, including me.

'So,' said Ms Dorrit sternly, 'make the most of it.'

That's exactly what I'm doing, Doug.

I worked on the idea all day at school, and as soon as I got home I put it to Dad.

'Invite Mr Grimmond to the swimming carnival,' I said. 'Then, after I've won the diving and he's mega impressed and wants to be my friend, we can tell him about my future diving career and how I'm available for sponsorship.'

As Dad put his cup of tea down he knocked the spoon out of the sugar bowl so I could tell he was interested.

'If the bank's sponsoring me and I'm gunna be getting them top publicity all over the world,' I said, 'they're not gunna sack you, are they? Plus if I offer to put their logo on my swimmers I reckon they'll be nicer to the folks round here.'

'Brilliant,' said Gran.

Dad didn't say anything.

Mum put her hand gently on my arm.

'What if you don't win the diving, love?' she said.

I didn't want to mention your name, Doug, and get Dad ropeable again.

So I just tried to look very confident.

'I can do it,' I said. 'I know I can.'

'He'll have a punt,' said Gran. 'You can't ask more than that.'

Mum didn't look convinced.

Dad didn't say anything.

My insides sagged.

Then Mum put her hand on Dad's arm.

'Wouldn't hurt, Noel, would it?' she said. 'If Mr Grimmond sees what a top little community we've got here, he might be easier on all of us.'

Dad thought about it.

'Worth a punt,' he said.

Gran nearly choked on her tea.

I've just done a few practice dives off the wardrobe and I haven't lost the knack, Doug.

So I won't need to bother you again till I'm up on the diving board tomorrow.

This is gunna be the best day of my whole life, I just know it, Doug.

It is so far, and I've only been awake four seconds.

When I opened my eyes, the first thing I spotted was Grandad's medal on my pillow.

I stared at the gleaming metal diver soaring over the writing and my insides soared too.

Then I glanced out the window.

I don't reckon I'd have known for sure what I was seeing if Dad hadn't been yelling in the front yard.

'Clouds! Clouds!'

I'm dragging on my swimmers and rushing outside.

Jeez, there's lots of them.

Ten, fifteen, twenty at least.

They're huge.

One of them's covering the sun.

There's one that looks like Gran blowing smoke out of her ear.

Doug, you're a genius.

Everyone's out in the street in their pyjamas, pointing and shouting.

And arguing.

Daryl the postie's telling Gran clouds don't mean anything, there were clouds here six years ago and they were dry as a wombat's wellies.

Gran's telling him not to be such a misery.

I reckon she knows, Doug.

Even though she has spells when she loses her grip, I reckon she knows you're on the job and you're gunna crack it.

She's offering to lend Daryl her umbrella.

Daryl's getting so worked up he's not even paying attention to his job.

He's just lobbed a letter into our postbox and missed and now it's blowing across the front yard.

I'd better grab it.

I hope this isn't gunna be the worst day of my whole life.

It was going great until a minute ago.

Everyone in town's come to the swimming carnival.

I know that's probably so they could get out of work and stare up at the clouds, but at least they're here.

Most important of all, Mr Grimmond's here with Mum and Dad and Gran.

That's him down there in the suit and tie telling Gran he doesn't want a chocolate crackle.

Nobody's staring up at the clouds now, but.

They're staring up at me.

And pointing and yelling and carrying on.

They've been doing it ever since Ms Dorrit announced the diving would be first and I jumped up and sprinted for the diving board.

I didn't wait for her to explain that the diving would have to be off the side because the water's too shallow to use the high board.

I jumped on the ladder and started climbing up before anyone could stop me.

I was gunna wait till I reached the board before I gave you a hoi to watch out for me, Doug. You know, so I could dive without hitting the bottom and having my brains leak out into the pool.

I'm not there yet but I've just realised something.

It's such a dopey thing to have done, I'm almost ashamed to admit it.

I've got Gran's letter in my swimmers.

When I picked it up in the front yard earlier Gran was busy yelling at Daryl the postie. She gets really irate if she's interrupted when she's arguing, so I stuck the letter down my swimmers for safe keeping.

And forgot it.

Until now.

I don't know what to do.

The envelope's got a window in it so I can tell it's important.

If I dive it'll get sodden.

If I leave it on the board it'll blow away.

Mr Tristos and the other teachers are climbing the ladder.

I'm on the board now, but I can't think straight with the noise of the kids down there cheering and the parents yelling.

I'm opening the letter. I'm reading it so at least I can tell Gran what was in it.

Except it isn't a letter, it's a receipt.

From a transport company.

To Gran.

Thanking her for the money.

The money for the three tankers of water.

Oh, Jeez.

Doug, I need to know something really quickly now because Mr Tristos is nearly halfway up the ladder.

Did you make Gran send the water?

Or did she do it all by herself?

I'm confused, Doug, and I don't want to be.

I've got a crook feeling in my guts and it's not just cause I scraped my tummy on a step climbing up.

I need to know it was you who sent the water, Doug.

I need to know you're still looking after me.

It's urgent.

I'm on a very high diving board.

I've never done a high dive before into real water.

The water's a long way down and there isn't enough of it.

Mum and Dad are sitting down there with Mr Grimmond and everyone's depending on me.

I've got to dive.

Tell me you're still looking after me, Doug.

Mr Tristos has only got six steps left to climb.

Give me a sign, Doug.

Anything'll do.

A bird winking at me.

A cloud in the shape of a thumbs up.

Only three steps left.

I've got to dive now.

That black cloud over on the horizon looks a bit like a thumbs up.

Either that or a tombstone.

I guess I'll know in about five secs.

See ya, Doug.

Arms ... legs ... focus ...

Mr Tristos is so close I can feel drops of his sweat splashing on me.

Wait a sec.

148

Those drops.
They aren't from Mr Tristos.
They're from the sky.

RRRRRRRRRRRRRRRRRRRRRRRR
AAAAAAAAAAAAAAAAAAAAAAAAA
IIIIIIIIIIIIIIIIIIIIIIIIIIIIIIIIIIIIIIIIIIIIIIIIII
NNNNNNNNNNNNNNNNNNNNNNNN
!!

I would have dived, Doug.

I wanted to.

OK, at first I just wanted to stand there with my head back and feel the rain splashing on my face while my legs stopped wobbling.

But I got the urge to dive again after a few secs.

Once Mr Tristos started hugging me and dancing round on the board and singing.

Trouble was, I couldn't get back to the edge because the more Mr Tristos's clothes got sodden with rain, the heavier he was to drag.

And when Mrs Chaplin finally made it to the top and he let go and started dancing with her, so many ecstatic people down below had jumped into the pool there wasn't a clear patch of water.

I'm not complaining, Doug.

Now it's raining there'll be heaps of water to dive into.

Thanks to you.

And this time I'm gunna make it up to you, Doug.

For doubting you.

I'm gunna make sure everyone knows you're the hero who broke the drought.

I've told as many people as I can, Doug.

I'm not sure it sank in with everyone.

Sometimes it's hard to get people's attention when they're doing cartwheels in puddles and dancing on car roofs and kissing pot plants, but I did my best.

I got some people's attention, but.

They didn't actually say anything when I told them about your angel powers, but I could see they were impressed.

And grateful, Doug.

Like me.

I'd forgotten how noisy rain is.

Which is another reason why I'm having trouble getting some people's attention.

For example, in the car going out to the airstrip I told Dad, Mum, Gran and Mr Grimmond from the bank that you'd made it rain, Doug.

Nobody said a thing.

The noise of the rain must have drowned out my words.

Funny but, when we got to the airstrip and

Dad told Mr Grimmond that the farmers would soon be able to pay their debts and Mr Grimmond told Dad to keep up the good work and Dad told Mr Grimmond to hurry up or his plane might not be able to take off, the rain didn't drown out their words.

Oh well.

Perhaps I've strained my voice with too much yelling for joy.

I gave Gran her receipt when we got home.

It was pretty soggy, but she knew what it was.

I didn't say anything about you making her spend her life savings, Doug, in case she got irate and choked on her toast.

I just told her she's the best Gran in the whole world and gave her a hug.

She didn't say anything at first, just hugged me back.

Then she said, 'We're quits now, eh?'

I smiled and nodded even though I didn't understand what she meant.

She must have seen I didn't.

'I got you started on Doug,' she said, 'so I reckoned it was up to me to finish it. I reckoned the best way to convince you Doug isn't real was to fill the pool myself and prove you don't need him.'

I stared at her.

'I thought I couldn't survive without Grandad once,' she said, 'but I can.'

'Gran,' I said quietly, 'Doug is real. He made it rain.'

She started going on about low pressure fronts and high pressure fronts colliding in the upper atmosphere.

Poor old Gran.

People that kind-hearted shouldn't have to suffer the indignity of losing their grip and going unintelligible.

Mum and Dad and Gran have been explaining that it takes twenty-four hours of heavy rain for water to start soaking in to drought-struck land.

They reckon it'd be well and truly doing that now, Doug.

'I reckon those paddocks'll be almost as waterlogged as you soon,' Gran's just said.

I'm in the bath.

I don't mind her being here, but.

I've got the water so deep she can't see anything.

Two days of non-stop rain.

You're a genius, Doug.

Dad reckons the farmers' dams are filling and there are green shoots coming up at the Wilkinsons' place.

That's what he overheard at the Gas 'N' Gobble.

The farmers aren't actually speaking to him yet, but they will be soon now he's off their backs.

And once the rain stops and we have the swimming carnival and my diving career takes off, he'll be a hero.

Three days.

Doug, this is wonderful.

I had no idea you'd do it this well.

The river's flowing really fast now.

I'd forgotten this town even had a river.

We had a class excursion down there today and I tried to get everyone to sign a petition.

When I've got a hundred signatures I'll present it to the council.

It's to get the name changed from the Strathpine River to the Doug River.

Not many of the kids wanted to sign it today, but that was probably because the rain was making the letters go runny.

Four days.

Boy, Doug, when you break a drought you really break a drought.

PE was cancelled today because the school hall roof's leaking.

On the way home I went to the video store for Gran, and guess what?

Mr Bullock's cleared out his Water section.

Now it's called Sun and Sand.

Troy and Brent Malley were there picking up *Desert Killers* for their folks.

When I asked them to sign the petition they got really nervous and stood very close to Mr Bullock.

Troy said he'd give me half a Mars Bar if I'd leave them alone.

Pretty weird, eh?

Mum reckons rain can affect people like that.

Five days of rain.

Unbelievable.

Actually Doug, five days will probably be enough.

We probably won't need much more rain after today.

You know, given that all the dams are full.

And all the water tanks have been overflowing for three days.

And there are seven trucks bogged on the highway outside town.

And Gran's muesli has started sprouting.

Don't get me wrong, Doug, we're very grateful.

But today's probably the last day we'll need rain as such.

~

Doug, I know you like to do a job really well.

That's why you're the world's number one angel.

Well you've done this job really, really well.

Six days non-stop rain is a top effort.

But it's definitely enough.

OK?

Thanks.

Emergency call to Doug.

The main street's under water.

So's the front yard.

It's started coming into the house.

Stop the rain, Doug.

Please.

This is an urgent message to Doug's secretary.

If he's off saving a school camp from a killer spider or something, could you let him know that the rain he started on the Mitch Webber job eight days ago has got totally out of hand.

Gran's bed is soaked.

I've had to put everything in my room on top of the wardrobe.

Mum's had to put all the money at the bank into plastic bags.

The town's being evacuated.

Get him back here.

Now.

~

I don't understand, Doug.

Where are you?

Can't you see what's happening?

Or is the rain getting in your eyes too?

The whole town's queueing up to get into army helicopters.

Everyone's wet and muddy and miserable.

Most of the grown-ups have been up for the last two nights filling sandbags to try and stop the river bursting its banks.

They've had to give up.

There's a heap of water on its way down from up north and there's just not enough sandbags in town.

Even if we used bags of sheep pellets and disposable nappies we couldn't stop it.

So we're all standing here on the sports oval up to our knees in water.

Nobody's saying anything, but I can tell what everyone's thinking.

The same as me.

Why have you abandoned us, Doug?

Looks like me and Dad are history.

Dunno why I'm even telling you this, Doug.

Habit, I guess.

At least it gives my brain something to do instead of panic.

Brains don't panic as much when they're up to their necks in work.

That's what Gran reckons.

I'm gunna listen to her more from now on.

I reckon I should have listened to her more when she was trying to tell me about you.

Anyway, I've listened to her about brains, which is why I gave mine a job to do while we were waiting for the helicopters to arrive.

I made it try to cheer me up and make me forget about the rain running down the back of my neck by thinking that at least Carla wasn't in my queue saying 'I told you.'

Then I looked at the other queues.

She wasn't in any of those either.

'Dad,' I said, 'Carla and her mum aren't here.'

Dad looked at me with a grim wet face.

'Neither are the Wilkinsons or the Malleys,' he said, 'but we can't worry about them, Mitch, we've got our own problems.'

I looked at him and Mum and Gran.

The only problems I could see were that Dad's green garbage bag raincoat was a hopeless fit and Mum was sad about leaving her computer and dartboard behind and Gran was grumpy because she'd spent all her savings on water and now we were up to our knees in it.

'Should have spent it on beer,' she was muttering.

I told Dad about Carla's mum's ute and how it never started properly if condensation got into the carby.

'That's just a few drops of water,' I said. 'Imagine what a flood'll do.'

'Mitch,' said Dad, 'forget it.'

I couldn't.

'Carla's mum wanted to buy a new ute,' I said, 'but the bank wouldn't lend her the money.'

Dad looked like he wished he was somewhere else.

Africa or somewhere.

Then he had a muttered conversation with Mum.

Mum nodded.

Gran slapped him on the back.

I was so dazed at seeing this that I was slow off the mark when Dad started sloshing his way across the oval.

'Wait,' I yelled, splashing after him. 'I'm coming too.'

He started to send me back, then something made him change his mind.

Perhaps he thought if I came, Doug, you'd be coming too.

Big joke.

We went over to where Dad had tied the four-wheel drive to the war memorial with the winch cable to stop it being swept away.

Dad untied it and we headed out of town towards Carla's place.

The road was hard to see under the water but Dad knows the district like the back of his clipboard so we were right.

For a while.

Then I noticed something.

The water wasn't just splashing up onto the bullbar any more, sometimes it was foaming over the bullbar onto the bonnet.

'Slow down,' I said to Dad.

'We're only doing twenty k's,' said Dad. 'It's not us.'

I knew what he meant.

The water was getting deeper.

Normally at that stage I'd have asked you to

160

keep an eye on us Doug, but there didn't seem much point.

Instead I tried to keep Dad's spirits up.

'These four-wheel drives are great, aren't they?' I said. 'The way they keep going through anything.'

Dad grunted.

The engine coughed.

The four-wheel drive stopped.

Dad's been out there fiddling under the bonnet and swearing for ages now.

I've been up on the roof for a squiz around but all I could see was water.

The rain's stopped but the water's still rising.

Another third of a gearstick and it'll be over the car seat.

I blame myself.

I should never have got Dad to try and do a rescue.

Oh well, Doug.

Or Doug's secretary.

Or Doug's answering machine.

Or whoever's listening.

If anyone is.

Which I doubt.

At least Carla's not here to say 'I told you.'

'I told you.'

As soon as I heard Carla's voice I spun round.

And banged my head on the roof of the car.

I'd forgotten I was sitting on the back of the seat.

My eyes went funny for a bit and I could have sworn there was a boat coming towards us.

A blue and yellow boat.

With a huge outboard motor.

And a highly trained State Emergency Service rescue team.

Then my eyes cleared and I saw what it really was.

A blue and yellow boat.

With two oars flapping.

And two people arguing.

'I told you we were going the right way,' Carla was shouting. 'There's Mitch's dad's four-wheel drive. We must be close to town.'

'So where are the houses?' yelled Carla's mum. 'Where's the Gas 'N' Gobble?'

After me and Dad finished telling them how pleased we were to see them and we climbed into the boat, and Mrs Fiami finished scowling and moved some kitchen utensils to make room, and Dad knocked one of the oars into the water and I grabbed it, and Dad sat down and knocked the other oar into the water and Carla grabbed it, Mrs Fiami sighed.

'My late husband was a fisherman,' she said. 'He'd have got us to town easy peasy.'

Dad stood up and knocked a frying pan into the water.

'Sorry,' he said.

I grabbed at it, but it sank.

Dad peered at the row of fence posts sticking out of the water.

'We go that way,' he said.

Mrs Fiami showed us how the oars worked.

She and Carla took one.

Me and Dad took the other.

We started rowing.

Dad soon got the hang of it and we stopped going round in circles and headed off in the direction he told us.

Why am I telling you this, Doug?

When you're not even listening?

Just to let you know that we can look after ourselves, thank you very much.

The Wilkinsons were amazed to see us, partly because they're both over seventy and they don't get many visitors, and partly because of the boat.

'Amazing,' said Mr Wilkinson as we helped him off his roof. 'Don't see many of these little beauties this far from the sea.'

'I hate it,' said Mrs Fiami.

'Are you keen on fishing?' asked Mrs Wilkinson as Dad lifted her into the boat.

'I hate it,' said Mrs Fiami.

She explained she'd only kept the boat as evidence. Something to do with Mr Fiami's life insurance and a mongrel insurance company.

While Dad explained to the Wilkinsons that there wasn't room for all their carpets and chickens, I had a word to Carla.

She'd hardly made a sound since we got in the boat and I could see she was upset about something.

'Is it Roald and Enid,' I asked quietly, 'and the others?'

Sheep hate water even more than mayors do.

Carla shook her head.

'They're on our roof with the last of the feed,' she mumbled. 'They'll be right.'

She bit her lip.

'We left the photo album behind,' said Mrs Fiami sadly.

Carla's eyes glinted.

'With the only photos of her dad,' continued Mrs Fiami. She gave a sigh. 'It's probably history by now.'

Carla looked away.

I didn't know what to say.

Dad stood up and knocked a hall rug into the water.

'Sorry,' he said.

He peered at the fence posts.

'The Malleys' place is this way,' he said.

I thought of you, Doug, and how quickly you'd get us out of this.

Then I grabbed an oar and tried to think of a way to tell Carla that I know how she feels about being dumped.

The Malleys were amazed to see us too.

They stood on their roof and aimed rifles at us.

'Don't you bank buggers ever give up?' snarled Mr Malley.

Dad explained it wasn't an eviction, it was a rescue.

Mr Malley didn't look impressed.

Mrs Malley told Troy and Brent to stop snivelling.

Troy and Brent both went bright pink because they'd been hoping me and Carla wouldn't notice.

When they all got into the boat I could still see tears on Troy and Brent's cheeks.

While Dad explained to Mr and Mrs Malley that there wasn't room for all their guns, I gave Troy and Brent a sympathetic look.

'We'd have been OK,' mumbled Troy, 'if Dad hadn't accidentally shot the fuel line in the ute.'

Mrs Malley cuffed him round the head.

Dad stood up and knocked a double-barrelled shotgun into the water.

Mr Malley howled.
Dad didn't say anything.
He just squinted at the fence posts.
We're on our way to town now.

The boat started leaking about halfway there.

Not a lot at first, but then more.

'It's the planks,' said Mrs Fiami. 'Some of them are a bit rotten.'

Everyone grabbed kitchen utensils and started scooping the water out.

Except me.

I'd had a thought.

A top fisherman like Mr Fiami must have kept stuff in his boat to repair leaks.

Plastic sealant and stuff.

I had a hunt around under people's feet.

Then Dad gave a yell.

The metal thing that kept his oar in place had popped out of the wood.

Mr Wilkinson grabbed it before it could fall in the water.

'There's a brick somewhere to knock it back in,' said Mrs Fiami. 'In the cabin, Mitch.'

I crawled into the little cabin and found the brick.

It was dirty pink with black bits.

I passed it down to Dad and hoped he wouldn't notice.

Then I realised Carla had been crouching next to me the whole time.

She took a deep breath and cleared her throat.

'When the bank wouldn't lend us money to buy feed,' she said quietly, 'I got very ropeable.'

She glanced nervously at me, and then at Dad, who was banging the metal thing in with the brick.

Dad looked like a man who was worrying about saving ten people from drowning, not worrying about broken windows from the past.

'Sorry,' said Carla softly.

I squeezed her arm to let her know I'd have done the same thing if my dad had drowned and my sheep were starving.

Then I saw something.

Behind Carla's head.

A sort of hole in the cabin wall.

It wasn't a rotten hole, it was a cut hole.

The sort of hole a person would make if they were looking for somewhere to store tubes of plastic sealant and their boat didn't have any drawers.

I stuck my hand in there, hoping it wasn't where Mr Fiami had stored the fish guts.

It wasn't.

Inside I felt something hard and square.

After a bit of juggling I lifted out a metal box that looked exactly like a tool box.

It was locked with a padlock.

Jeez, I thought, this must be really expensive plastic sealant.

Carla tapped me on the shoulder and handed me the brick.

For a sec I thought she was offering it to me to keep and chuck through her window when the flood was over.

Then I twigged.

I started whacking the padlock with it.

After a few whacks, the padlock broke and the lid flipped open.

Inside the box were some small metal hooks and a plastic bag and some sort of pistol.

Carla opened the bag.

I examined the pistol but it wasn't a sealant gun.

The plastic bag didn't have sealant in it either, just an old notebook.

'Mitch, Carla,' yelled Dad. 'Bail out some of this water or we won't make it.'

We've been scooping water for hours.

That's why I'm telling you all this, Doug or the man in the moon or whoever's listening, to take my mind off the pain in my arms.

And to block out Troy and Brent's sobbing.

And to let you know we are gunna make it.

I just want to say, Doug or the man in the moon or whoever, that we would have made it.

If it hadn't been for the tidal wave.

When we reached town it was almost dark, but we could still see the roofs in the main street.

I felt like cheering, even though I had blisters from rowing and arm cramps from scooping.

Then Mrs Malley screamed.

For a sec I thought she'd seen a relative or a helicopter with dry towels on board.

Then Mr Malley screamed.

So did Troy, Brent and the Wilkinsons.

I spun round.

Moving towards us from the direction of the river, faster than ten cattle trucks having a drag, was a wall of water.

Roofs were disappearing under it.

'Hang on!' yelled Dad, and then it hit us.

Suddenly we were powering down the main street so fast that if Sergeant Crean had been on board we'd have been booked for sure.

And then just as suddenly it had gone, and we were left spinning round and round, all still screaming.

I opened my eyes.

The main street had gone too.

The only bit of town I could see was the diving board tower.

Water was pouring into the boat.

'Row,' yelled Dad. 'Head for the diving board.'

We all rowed frantically using oars, saucepans, rifles and hands.

Somehow we got there.

Dad made us all clamber onto the steps before he'd leave the boat.

For a sec I thought he'd left it too late.

'Dad!' I screamed as the boat sank.

Dad jumped for the steps.

He clanged onto them.

Once the steps had stopped shaking, and we had too, we climbed slowly up to the top.

Diving boards aren't made for ten people, so it's pretty crowded up here.

We're just sort of huddled together in the dark, listening for helicopters.

We haven't heard any yet, but they could

171

have been drowned out by Troy and Brent's sobbing and Mrs Wilkinson's asthma.

And the noise of the water swirling past.

The diving board gives a shudder every now and then.

I haven't said anything, but I keep thinking about how crumbly the concrete is at the base of the steps.

I think Dad might be thinking about that too, because he muttered something a while back.

He had his arms round me, and he must have forgotten his mouth was so close to my ears.

'OK Doug,' he said, 'I give in. Get us out of this and I'll believe in you.'

I've been holding my breath for ages.

But you're not getting us out of it, are you, Doug?

We're on our own, aren't we?

Well stuff you, Doug.

You had your chance and you blew it.

Now I'm gunna save us.

I just wish I didn't have to dive into that dark swirling water.

If I can hold my breath long enough to get down to the kiosk and back, I'll be right.

If.

Best not to think about it, as Gran says when she's eating tripe.

Stand up quickly before Dad realises what's going on.

Arms.

Legs.

Quick focus.

And dive.

Oh no, my head's too far back.

My tummy's sticking too far out.

I'm doing a belly fl—

I must have blacked out.

The belly flop must have winded me.

I don't get it.

I'm in the water, but I'm not sinking.

I can feel the current dragging at my feet, but I'm not moving.

What's this round my chest?

Arms.

Strong arms.

I can hardly breathe.

Doug?

You at last?

Is that you whispering in my ear?

Telling me I'm a stupid maniac?

No.

It's Dad.

He wants to know if I'm ok.

I can't speak.

Partly because Dad's squeezing so hard.

Partly because I'm crying.
Funny thing with us humans, Doug.
Mostly we cry when we're sad.
But sometimes we cry when we're happy.

I've just told Dad my plan.

'The Stegnjaaics' old inflatable plastic swimming pool,' I said. 'If nobody's shifted it from where I left it, it's down there in the kiosk with all the empty plastic bottles. We could use it as a raft.'

Dad sighed and I felt his hot breath on my ear.

'It's got a huge rip in it,' he said. 'I checked it out the day the Stegnjaaics dumped it at the tip.'

We're floating in the blackness.

While Dad treads water I'm trying to think of another plan.

I can't.

My brain hasn't got another plan in it.

Not to save Dad.

Not to save anyone.

Not even to save me.

Suddenly drowning doesn't seem so bad after all.

Me and Dad, together.

Hang on.

Dad's body has just gone rigid.

'Empty plastic bottles?' he's saying. 'What empty plastic bottles?'

Dad's a hero.

The Malleys and the Wilkinsons have been going round the campsite telling everyone how Dad saved us.

How he kept diving down into the pool kiosk and coming up with empty plastic bottles.

How he made us stuff the bottles inside our clothes until we could float.

How he tied us all together with strips of inflatable plastic swimming pool and towed us away from the diving board just before it collapsed.

OK, they reckon I'm a bit of a hero too.

I've tried to explain to everyone it was just luck that I'd stuffed the pistol from the boat down my shorts.

And luck that I had the idea of firing it while we were floating to attract attention.

And luck that it turned out to be a flare gun.

But people don't believe me.

Specially as Troy and Brent Malley are going round telling the other kids it wasn't luck, it was my guardian angel.

Mum's just tried to make me lie down in one of the army tents and get some sleep, but I don't feel like it cause I'm still too excited after being in the helicopter.

Plus it's too noisy to sleep with all those frogs making such a din.

Plus there's too much going on.

Mum understands cause she's pretty excited too.

She's got the plastic bags of bank money and she's giving a personal loan to whoever needs one, which is something she's always wanted to do.

I've been hugging Dad and Mum and Gran for about an hour.

Gran's spent a lot of that time gazing proudly at Dad, which I think is making him a bit nervous.

When Dad was voted chairman of the town clean-up committee, for a sec I thought Gran was going to call the newspapers.

Mr Bullock was behaving as though he wanted the job, until he saw Gran looking at him.

Then he backed away, though that could have been because Gran had just taken a drag on her cigarette and a mouthful of army biscuit.

Dad's just been explaining to everyone about government flood relief payments and how they're always more than drought relief.

While everyone was cheering, Dad put his arm round me.

He bent down and I thought it was for another hug.

It wasn't just for that.

'He's quite a bloke,' whispered Dad, 'your Doug.'

Why am I telling you all this, Doug?

Because in the helicopter I finally understood what you've been up to.

It started when I apologised to Carla.

'You were right,' I said. 'It was angel bull.'

She grinned, and her eyes were softer and happier than I'd ever seen.

'No, it wasn't,' she said.

And she opened the plastic bag from the boat and showed me the old notebook.

Her dad's notebook.

Carla wouldn't show me what was in it, but every time she peeked inside her eyes glowed softer so I reckon it must have been about her.

'If Doug hadn't made it rain so much,' she said quietly, 'I'd never have found this.'

I stared at her while everything sank in.

Carla hugged the notebook and smiled again.

'I've had a guardian angel all along,' she said.

So have I, Doug.
He's over there with his arm round Mum.
Thank you.

Morris Gleitzman
Water Wings

Pearl and Gran dragged the boxes of junk out of the attic. Sticking out of Pearl's box were some fat pink tubes. She picked one up and realized what it was.

"Gran," she said. "Are these floaties yours?"

"They're water wings," Gran said. She stared at the water wings for ages. Her eyes, Pearl saw, were full of tears.

Pearl has a secret hidden in the family freezer, but Gran's dark secrets are buried much deeper. Pearl, Gran and Winston the guinea pig face some tough truths in this brilliant, funny and moving novel from the author of *Two Weeks with the Queen*.

'Will make you laugh and cry.' *Young Telegraph*

Morris Gleitzman
Misery Guts

Keith's heart was pounding. Calm down, he thought. You're not robbing a bank. You're not kidnapping anybody. You're just painting a fish and chip shop orange.

Keith is trying to cheer up his parents. But a pair of misery guts need more than a pot of Tropical Mango Hi-Gloss to make them happy. What they really need, Keith decides, is to live in Paradise.

Trouble is, Paradise is halfway round the world.

Even Keith Shipley is stumped by that one. Almost.

'Totally compelling.' *Children's Books of the Year*

'Great fun.' *Books for Keeps*

Morris Gleitzman
Worry Warts

Dear Mum and Dad,

This is just to let you know that I took the torch, the hammer, the gardening trowel, the plastic strainer, the chocolate biscuits and the stuff that's missing from the bathroom. So it's OK, you haven't been burgled. Please don't worry, things are looking even better than I thought, opal-wise.

Love, Keith

Going down a mine and digging up a fortune in precious opals is Keith's solution to his parents' problems. Stacks of money will make everything OK in their tropical paradise, and save them from being permanent worry warts.

Won't it?

Another brilliant Keith Shipley plan – if it works . . .

Morris Gleitzman titles
available from Macmillan

The prices shown below are correct at the time of going to press.
However, Macmillan Publishers reserve the right to show new retail
prices on covers which may differ from those previously advertised.

MORRIS GLEITZMAN

Misery Guts	0 330 32440 3	£3.99
Worry Warts	0 330 32845 X	£3.99
Puppy Fat	0 330 34211 8	£3.99
Blabber Mouth	0 330 39777 X	£4.99
Sticky Beak	0 330 39778 8	£4.99
Belly Flop	0 330 39824 5	£4.99
Water Wings	0 330 39825 3	£4.99

All Macmillan titles can be ordered at your local bookshop
or are available by post from:

Book Service by Post
PO Box 29, Douglas, Isle of Man IM99 1BQ

Credit cards accepted. For details:
Telephone: 01624 675137
Fax: 01624 670923
E-mail: bookshop@enterprise.net

Free postage and packing in the UK.
Overseas customers: add £1 per book (paperback)
and £3 per book (hardback).